W9-CHR-516

CUTS LIKE

A KNIFE

JOYCE A SMITH

STORY TELLING PUBLISHER

CUTS LIKE A KNIFE

JOYCE A SMITH

This novel is a work of fiction. Any resemblance to real people, either living or dead, actual events, establishments, organizations or locale are entirely coincidental, and are intended to give the fiction a sense of reality and authenticity. Other names, characters, places or incidents are either products of the author's imagination, or are used fictitiously as are those fictitious events and incidents that involve real persons did not occur or are set in the future.

Note: Sale of this book without a cover is unauthorized. If this book is purchased without a cover, it may have been reported to the publisher as "unsold or destroyed." Neither the author nor the publisher may have received payment for the sale of this book.

Library of Congress Control Number (LCCN): 2016907214

Fiction: Contemporary

ISBN: 9780-997347500

Published by Story Telling Publishers, Printed in the USA, First Edition - Paperback and Electronic
No part of this book can be reproduced in any form, except for the inclusion of brief quotations in a review, without permission in writing from the author and publisher.

ACKNOWLEDGEMENTS

First, I give honor and glory to the Almighty for keeping me on course and giving me the strength to keep going when I wanted to give up.

It took many years and a great amount of encouragement for me to complete this book. I thank my husband, Andre Smith, a reader, cover photographer, and supporter; my son, Charles Turner; my sister, Ellen Perry read and gave advice, grandchildren, and all my other family members and friends for their encouragement and support.

A Special thanks is given to Dorothy J Morris, author of "Fatal Rebounds and Fatal Vengeance", who worked diligently and put in countless hours to edit my book. In the early stages, Stella Adams, author of "Heavy is the Rain" and Wanda Kimball were on the ground floor helping lay the foundation. Stella came back as a final reader.

Thank you to Irene Woods, Marsha Vaughn, Diane Sexton, and Joanne Partee who took time out of their busy schedules to read and make suggestions.

Thank you to James Jones, of Jimi Jones Visual for the book cover.

Thank you in advance to those of you who purchase this book. May this book inspire hope and community participation in my beloved City of Baltimore.

This Book is Dedicated to My Husband and Loving Family

CHAPTER 1

It had been a rough night, and Asia Wallace sought comfort by getting into her mother's bed and hugging the pillow. The young girl went into the closet, turned on the overhead light, and closed the door. She crouched on the floor and stroked her mother's favorite fur coat until she heard voices. The twelve-year-old realized it was her father, and her mother's identical twin sister, talking in the bedroom. Asia turned off the dim overhead light, peeped through a small crack in the closet door, and listened to them.

"Where've you been? Mike called from the hospital a couple of hours ago," Brenda said as she wrapped her arms around Asia's father.

"Linda's dead, now we don't have to hide anymore since she's gone. Walter, you love me?"

"Yes, I love you, but good grief your sister is dead. Was Asia at the hospital when her mother passed?"

"No, my brother sent her home; she'd been there the whole night."

"We'll still need to be cool for a little while," Walter said removing himself from Brenda's embrace. "Asia doesn't even know her mother's gone, and I'll need to spend some time with my daughter."

Brenda threw up her hands and shouted, "When did you ever give a damn for your daughter, or anybody but yourself?"

"Good question," Mike roared, bursting into the bedroom. "I had a feeling something wasn't right with you two. Both of you get the hell out of my house!"

Walter stood still and crossed his arms. "If I leave, I'm taking my daughter with me."

"Take her where?" Mike blasted. "Walter, you ain't got nothing, and nowhere to take her. Trust and believe you're not taking my niece out of her home."

"That's the grief talking, don't make me hurt you," Walter said as he pushed Mike against the wall, knocking over the clock sitting on top of the dresser.

Mike pounced back, hit Walter in the face, and knocked him to the floor.

"Don't hurt him," Brenda screamed as she jumped in front of her brother to stop him from kicking Walter in the face.

Mike glared at her. "Brenda, you disgust me. Linda was your twin sister." He pointed his finger, and yelled; "Both of you get out of here and don't come back."

Her mother was dead. Asia covered her mouth with her shaking hands to keep from screaming, but it did not stop her tears from falling.

CHAPTER 2

Asia awoke from a fitful night's sleep on the thirteenth anniversary of her mother's death. She had an uneasy feeling in the pit of her stomach, and blamed it on the slice of pizza she ate before going to bed. Asia's three-year-old son, Eric, was getting his first haircut today, and the young woman knew her mother would go with them to the barbershop if she were alive.

"Git up Mommy!" Eric shouted as he barged into his mother's bedroom and dived on her bed. "Git up! You not sleep." Eric pried open one of her eyes with his little fingers and put his face close to hers. "I can see you Mommy. I git hair cut today. I gonna look hansem."

Asia opened her eyes, "Yes, you will look handsome," she corrected and looked into her son's small face looming above hers, with his grandmother's eyes.

"Yep, I be big boy. Come on Mommy, git up," he begged as he jumped on her bed.

"Boy, you better stop jumping on my bed," she said tickling him.

Eric laughed so hard it made Asia laugh, and it touched her heart to see her little boy happy.

"I love you this much, Mommy," Eric said as he held his little arms open.

"And I love you this much," Asia told him as she opened her arms playing their game. She looked at the clock beside her bed. "It's seven o'clock on a Saturday morning, my day to sleep longer."

"I have to get haircut," Eric pleaded before he jumped off her bed.

Asia watched her little boy dance around the bedroom singing a tune from his favorite movie, *The Lion King,* with the sun bouncing off his little brown body. Throwing back the covers, she said, "I'm getting up. Now, go downstairs and let Mommy get dressed."

Eric left her room, she wanted to go back to sleep, but knew if she was not up soon he would be back to bug her. She climbed out of the bed, headed to the bathroom, and looked in the mirror. Asia caressed her short curly hair and thought how letting Mr. Joe, the local barber, cut her hair was a good decision. Her hair was easy to care for and the cut was flattering.

Asia could smell the delicious scent of bacon cooking as she showered and dressed. She entered the kitchen several minutes later and found her aunt over the stove.

"Bout time you got up," Pearl said frying the last of the bacon. "This boy of yours gonna drive us crazy over getting his hair cut today."

"I smelled bacon upstairs, and I'm hungry." Asia poured a cup of coffee and sat at the kitchen table next to Eric. She admired the flowers from Pearl's garden sitting in a vase with the morning sun streaming on them as a spotlight.

Sipping her coffee, Asia observed her fifty-plus aunt singing along to gospel music playing on the radio. Pearl wore a bright pink sundress that showed off her smooth, pecan complexion on her size fourteen frame. She had her mixed gray hair in a ponytail, and her oblong shaped face free of makeup. Asia wondered how her aunt could look so nice this early in the morning.

"Can a man sleep in his own house?" Mike joked entering the kitchen and joining Asia and Eric at the table.

"Why is everyone up so early?" Asia asked. "It's Saturday."

"Ask your son," Pearl answered. "We can't sleep with him running around yapping about getting his hair cut?"

Mike stroked one of Eric's braids, "I'm glad you're taking him. It's time he looks like a boy instead of a girl with these long braids."

Pearl pointed her finger at Mike. "You're old-fashioned and don't want to see boys with long braids. It's 1996, boys today have long hair."

Mike poured a cup of coffee and sat at the table, "You're so right, I'm old-fashioned. These may be modern times, but boys should look like boys." He directed his attention to Asia, "Joe will do a good job cutting his hair. You know, his shop is one of the few businesses left that didn't move out when the government allowed this drug invasion."

"Oh, please don't start!" Pearl said, putting her hands on her hips.

Asia had heard her uncle tell stories of how Lafayette Heights once existed a million and a half times, and he would repeat the stories as if it were the first time he told them. She realized the worsening of their neighborhood was difficult for both her aunt and uncle, but it affected her uncle the most.

"You know it's true. Nothing this big or devastating happens without the government allowing it." Mike sipped his coffee. "Pearl; remember when Dr. Bryan and his family lived across the street, and the high-school teacher, Mrs. Owens, lived on the corner? Now, we have rows of boarded-up houses."

"I remember."

Mike continued his conversation, glancing at his wife. "Pearl, tell Asia how on each Saturday mornings everyone in the block got up early, washed the front steps, and polished the brass railings." He shook his head. "The railings are gone. Damn junkies stole them and sold them for money to buy drugs."

"She knows Mike, and watch your mouth in front of Eric."

"Today, we ain't going to deal with this drug business. My little man is getting his first haircut." Mike picked up his nephew, extended his six-foot frame with Eric in his arms, and gave the giggling child a big bear hug as Eric wrapped his arms around his great uncle's neck.

"Yep, Uncle Mike I git haircut today," Eric danced around the kitchen after his uncle put him down.

"I'm taking him after we eat breakfast," Asia smiled.

"Thank goodness," Mike and Pearl said in unison.

CHAPTER 3

Eric skipped and jumped as they headed to Joe's Sharpest Cuts to get his first haircut. Asia had to hold his hand to keep him from running ahead of her. She was also excited, but alert even on an early June Saturday morning. The enthusiastic mother and son crossed the street as they continued walking pass three little girls playing jump rope. Next to the playing children were two teenagers sitting on the steps drinking beer and listening to rap music blasting from a boom box.

"Hello, Mr. Joe," Asia said as she entered his barbershop.

"My goodness," Joe said as he lifted his large frame from his chair to greet Asia and her son. "Hi Eric, it's good to see you."

"Hi, Mr. Joe," Eric said. "I git haircut."

"You certainly will," Joe said laughing, as he prepared by placing a small box in the barber chair. Eric giggled as Joe propped him up on the box and made a ceremony out of putting the cape around his little neck. Asia sat across from them and watched her son get his braids cut; she wondered how many little boys had gotten their first haircuts in this barbershop.

Joe had the first chair closest to the door and the window. Colby, the second, and two other barbers used the third and fourth chairs. Across from the barbers, were several seats for patrons waiting for a haircut or sitting around as Joe often said, *"Shooting the breeze."*

Displayed on half of the wall behind the patrons' seats were framed news clippings of the slayings of Martin Luther King, Malcolm X, and Nelson Mandela's release from jail.

The other half of the wall was what Joe called, *"The Wall of Fame."* Asia loved looking at the framed signed black and white photographs of singers and other famous entertainers from the fifties through the seventies. It was nostalgic and filled her with pride.

She asked Eric's father, Harry Blake, if he would come to the barbershop and see his son get his first haircut. It would have been a nice surprise for Eric if Harry had been present.

"No crazy talk," Joe said glancing over his small-framed glasses sitting on his full face as he cautioned the barbers and two other men in the shop. "We have a handsome boy and a beautiful lady in our company."

Asia smiled as she recognized the two older men Joe referenced. They were in the shop every time she came to get a cut. She never saw either of them get haircuts, but they were always there engaging in the same discussions.

"Joe, remember when the Royal Theatre was the place to go on the Avenue?" The greyest and thinner of the men stated. "Man everybody that was anybody, played there."

"Yeah he remembers," answered the other man before Joe could. "Look at those pictures on the wall? Many of those people stayed at Joe's house with his father."

"Man those were the days, the Avenue was jumping back then. Balmore was sure nuff a tough spot to play; but if you could make it here, you could play anywhere in the world."

Joe was finishing Eric's hair, when Asia glanced out the front window and saw a black Mercedes parked in front of the barbershop. A large dark man exited the car and strutted toward the shop. The man had on lots of big flashy jewelry, a baggy sweat suit, and a pair of expensive sneakers. He was wearing large black Cazal sunglasses that blended into his dark face and had an air that made Asia apprehensive. The feeling she experienced when she woke up this morning returned.

She often stayed and talked with Joe if there were no other patrons waiting for him, but not today. Asia was uncomfortable about the man entering the shop and decided she should leave as soon as Joe finished cutting Eric's hair.

As the sweat suit wearing man reached to open the door, a teenager shouted something from across the street, and the man turned around. Asia saw the youngster pull a shiny object from his pocket, but she could not tell what it was.

"You ready to see the new you?" Joe asked as he handed Asia's son a small mirror.

Eric looked in the mirror and smiled. "Look at me, Mommy. I look good."

"Yes you do sweetie," Asia said turning from the window.

"Wait till Uncle Mike see me," Eric said grinning from ear to ear.

"Let's go show Aunt Pearl and Uncle Mike the new you," Asia said as she walked toward her son and bent to retrieve one of his braids for the baby book. She heard three loud blasts, and the front window of the shop shattered.

The earsplitting noise came from outside and Asia realized what she saw in the young man's hand was a gun. "Oh my God," she screamed, as she grabbed Eric, pulled him to the floor, and covered him with her body. Joe fell across her legs and his blood splattered on her and the floor.

There were three more shot, louder than the first three. Asia wondered if the jewelry clad sweat suit wearing man, entering the shop was also firing.

Seconds passed, and she did not hear any more shooting. Asia attempted to get up from the floor, but the weight of Joe's body on her legs made it impossible. Colby came from behind his chair and removed Joe off Asia. Everyone else was still hiding, covering their heads with their arms. Colby checked Joe's pulse, and found his employer was still alive but unconscious.

Asia sat up and pulled Eric close to her. She panicked after noticing blood on the front of his shirt. "Are you all right?" she asked as she held him in her arms.

Eric did not answer; he smiled and touched her face. He closed his eyes and his body went limp in her arms. Asia looked into his sweet face with his fresh haircut for signs of life. She checked his pulse---he was not breathing.

Asia gave him CPR. "Call an ambulance," she screamed between breaths. "Please call an ambulance!" She worked and worked on Eric, but he never responded. The police and the ambulance arrived and took the shop owner to the hospital. Asia sat on the floor holding and rocking her dead child.

***

Tommie Jenkins did not make it far in his Mercedes before several police cars were chasing him. He swerved in and out of traffic trying to get away. The police cars surrounded Tommie, pulled him out of his car, and threw him on the ground with their guns drawn.

After his arrest, Tommie waited in his jail cell to see the court commissioner for a bail hearing on murder, attempted murder, and several other charges. He buried his head in his hands: *no good deed goes unpunished.*

Joyce A. Smith

Taking weed to Colby in west Baltimore in exchange for haircuts was a big mistake, but they were friends and lost their jobs from Bethlehem Steel at the same time.

Colby was careful not to purchase his drugs from the local dealers selling around Joe's shop as he did not want his employer to know he was buying and smoking marihuana.

Tommie despaired over his present situation. He could not believe this was over a little *weed*.

16

CHAPTER 4

The description Asia gave of the teen matched Lamont Tyne, known on the streets as Mag Dog. He was one of the local drug dealers who operated around the barbershop and was still at large. Ms. Patty Lagrue, the young and tough Assistant State's Attorney was out for blood and vowed the police would find the child killer. Tyne would face prosecution and the death penalty. The police were on alert to find Lamont (Mad Dog) Tyne.

Patty wanted to make the city a safer place to live and prided herself on taking hardened offenders off the streets of Baltimore. She had prosecuted other cases in which children were victims, but Eric's case was different; this was personal. For the first time since becoming a prosecutor, she wondered if she was making a difference.

She sat in her office swirling a pen and recalled how she first met Asia about a year ago. Patty was conducting an interview in her office and the victim became sick and vomited in a wastebasket. After the interview had concluded, Patty carried the container to the restroom; a woman with the most beautiful hazel eyes Patty had ever seen approached her.

"Miss, where are you taking that pail?" the hazel-eyed woman asked.

"Someone became sick in it, and I'm taking it to the restroom."

"No, that's my job, it's my first day." The hazel-eyed woman said smiling as she took the wastebasket from Patty's hand.

"Who are you?"

"My name is Asia, and you'll mess up your pretty clothes."

The two women became friends, despite their social and employment differences. They found they had several things in common; both had lost their mothers at young ages and had issues with their fathers. Asia's demeanor reminded Patty of her grandmother. As the friendship continued to develop between the two women, the tough prosecutor began calling Asia's aunt and uncle, Aunt Pearl and Uncle Mike.

Patty's peers could not accept or understand her relationship with Asia. They accepted the friendship with Jay Bruce, her assistant, but not with someone on the janitorial staff.

The prosecutor stopped reminiscing, put down her pen, and walked into the reception room to retrieve case papers from Jay. Her office assistant looked up from the computer screen and smiled.

"How are you feeling Patty?"

"I'm okay, I guess. On top of everything else, today is the sixth-month anniversary of my late friend's death. First, Eleanor dies, and now this happens." Patty grimaced and shook her head before continuing. "I need to call her husband, check on him, and the kids.

She walked over to the window in the reception office and looked out the blinds. "My grandmother said death comes in threes. Hope it doesn't happen this time. I can't survive another death of someone I love. She also said you shouldn't try to put out a blazing fire with a thimble of water. I wonder if that's what I'm trying to do." Patty turned from the window. "Has the drug and crime situation in this city gotten so out of hand?"

"The alternative is to throw in the towel. I live in the city, and I'm glad you care." Jay nodded. "Thank goodness Jenkins is off the streets."

"Yeah, but I won't rest until Lamont Tyne is arrested. I had to make a concession with the boss to be the second prosecutor on this case because of my personal connection with Asia and Eric."

"You're going to be second chair? Who's first?"

"Richard Laws."

Jay frowned. "Richard, how are you going to handle him being first?"

"He's pompous, privileged, and only wants the notoriety that comes with prosecuting this case. Richard isn't the hardest worker and I'm not happy about this, but I'll make sure he does what's right."

"I know you will."

"After I leave work today, I plan to stop by Asia's house. Are you coming?"

"I need to pick up my daughter first, and then I'll be there."

"Okay, meet you there. I'm stopping home first."

***

The tough prosecutor left the courthouse and drove home agonizing over Eric's death. She lived in Bolton Ridge where doctors, lawyers, and other professionals still lived; Eric died five minutes away. Drugs had not invaded Patty's neighborhood in the same way it had Asia's community. There were consequences whenever crime crept into Bolton Ridge.

She changed her clothes, left her home, and headed to Asia's residence. Patty loved this formed-stoned home with its marble front steps, stained glass windows, and chandeliers; but today the house had a rather gloomy and somber atmosphere. Patty realized it was the first time she had come into this house and not smelled something cooking or heard music playing.

Mike and Pearl loved listening to different genres of music. They enjoyed jazz, reggae, R&B, gospel, and other forms. The variety of music brought back fond memories for Patty of sitting beside her father as he played the piano.

Pearl always had a pot of something good cooking on the stove. Patty would get hungry as soon as she walked through the front door and smelled the food even if she had just eaten. More than anything, she missed Eric running to her, wrapping his arms around her legs with a big smile across his face.

"Has Asia come out of her room?" Patty asked walking into the house.

"No," Pearl admitted, wringing her hands. "She hasn't been out since... I keep placing food outside her bedroom door, but when I go back later, the food is still there, untouched."

"She has to come out and eat something." Patty walked into the living room. "Hello Uncle Mike. How are you feeling?"

"It's my fault. I should've moved my family when everybody else left." He buried his face in his hands.

Patty placed her hand on his shoulder. "No, it's not your fault, Uncle Mike. I promise you, we have one suspect and we will get the other one. This is a top priority case."

"It won't bring my little man back. It won't bring him back," Mike said with a tear leaking from his eye.

"I know Uncle Mike," Patty sighed.

Minutes later, the doorbell rang, and Pearl opened the door. Jay and her daughter walked in the house and spoke to everyone. Kiki took out her crayons and coloring book from her bag, went into the dining room, and sat at the table. This was the first time Patty had seen Jay's child so quiet, and it was a pleasure. Patty thought

21

how different Eric was from Kiki and wanted to cry.

"I'm going upstairs to get Asia out of her room," Patty said. "Jay, can you help Aunt Pearl with the obituary?" She asked as she walked towards the stairs.

Before Jay could answer, the doorbell rang again. Pearl opened the door and Eric's father, pushed his way into the house. Harry was a thin man, but he pushed the door hard enough to cause Pearl to stumble backwards.

"Where's Asia? She let my son get killed." Harry screamed as he continued to push past Pearl.

"Are you crazy?" Mike jumped up from his seat and challenged Harry. "I know you're upset over your son, but don't disrespect my home. There're women and a child in here."

Harry's thin face contorted as he shouted back, "Asia is so stupid. How could she let his happen?"

"She didn't just let this happen," Mike responded. "Because of your sorry ass, she's been both mother and father to Eric. Where were you, when he got his first tooth, took his first step, or had the measles? She loved that child with all her heart." Mike pointed his finger at Harry. "Hell, where were you on Saturday when he got his first haircut? If you had been there, maybe you could've seen what was about to happen and protected them both, and you call yourself a man. Don't come into my home screaming and acting the fool!"

"You can't put this on me," Harry said. "I told Asia I wasn't ready to be a father. That's what's wrong with women. They think they can change a man."

"You'd have to be a man before Asia or anyone else could change you." Mike shouted.

Harry balled-up his fist, "Old man, I'll beat you until you pass out," Harry said as he charged toward Mike.

"Try it, you punk." Mike urged stepping towards Harry.

"Mike he's not worth it." Pearl grabbed Mike's arm, pulling him back, and attempting to calm him; but Mike continued moving towards Harry.

Patty had gone to the hall closet as soon as Harry entered the house. She removed her purse from the top shelf, took her gun out, and walked towards Eric's father. "I wouldn't do that if I were you," she said to him.

"And how you gonna stop...." Harry ceased talking and sweat broke out on his face as Patty aimed her 38 revolver at him.

"I prefer not to shoot you, but I will if you don't take your sorry ass out of here right this instant," she said through clenched teeth.

Harry left the house without a word. Patty put her gun back in her purse and returned it to the top shelf of the hall closet. She turned around and noticed everyone was still, and every eye was on her. She gave a weak smile and felt a little guilty as she noticed Kiki was in Jay's lap clinging to her mother.

"You're right; Asia has to come out of her room. I'll go to her, Patty. If I need help, I'll call you," Pearl said moving towards the staircase.

"I wish you had not stepped in," Mike said to Patty once Pearl reached the top of the stairs. "I think I could've taken that punk." Mike walked into the dining room and sat at the table. "Now we have to write an obituary while that idiot gets to play the broken-hearted father."

"It be okay Mr. Mike," Kiki said climbing out of her mother's lap, walking over, and holding her arms up to him.

"What in the world do you say on the obituary?" Mike's voice cracked as he picked up Kiki and placed her in his lap. "Do you mention Eric's first day at school he will never have, or his graduation from high school?" Mike took a deep breath and stroked Kiki's hair. "What about his first prom or getting his driving license, none of which will happen for Eric."

CHAPTER 5

Sitting on the floor outside Asia's bedroom door was a tray of untouched food. Pearl knocked on the door several times but there was no answer. She opened the door, and the odor of two days of grief hit her in the face. The room was dark, the blinds drawn, and the curtains closed. Pearl stood there trying to adjust to the darkness. She could not decide whether to open the curtains and the blinds, or turn on the lamp beside the red velvet love seat.

Pearl remembered the day Asia purchased this love seat from a thrift store. She would not let Asia bring it into the house and made Mike put it on the back porch. For three days, Pearl sprayed, washed, and prayed over the love seat. Mike told Pearl the spraying and washing made sense to get rid of any bugs or other critters, but the praying was nothing but the superstitions she had brought with her from Yellow Pond, South Carolina. Pearl did not care what Mike said, she had seen strange things happen in her time, and was not letting a piece of furniture in her home she had not done what she could to get rid of any possible bad attachments from the previous owners.

On the table beside the love seat, was the Thomas Blackshear sculpture Patty had given Asia of a boy giving his mother flowers. Pearl wondered if Asia could continue to cherish the sculpture or if seeing it would cause her pain. Pearl turned on the lamp and looked around the room. Even with the slight illumination from the lamp, the room was still dark. She looked at the bed on the other side of the room, but could not find Asia.

Pearl called her niece's name, but there was no answer. "Asia," she called again. There was still no answer. She continued to look around the room but could not find Asia. "Enough of this," Pearl said as she walked over to the window, opened the curtains and the blinds; and looked around the room again. She saw Asia sitting in the corner between the wall and the dresser, rocking and holding Eric's teddy bear. "Honey, you can't go on this way. Please get up from the floor," Pearl said kneeling beside her niece.

Asia continued to rock with the teddy bear in her arms. Pearl went to the bathroom and filled the tub with warm water and bubble bath. She returned to the bedroom and took Asia's hand, lifting her from the floor. She guided her niece to the bathroom and helped her take off her clothes and get into the tub. The broken-hearted woman did not show any facial expressions or make any sounds.

Pearl sang her favorite song, "Precious Lord" by Mahalia Jackson, as she washed Asia's back and arms. She stopped singing after she heard a low sound.

The noise stopped, and she continued singing, but it started again and grew louder. Pearl peeped out the bathroom window to make sure a small animal was not in the back yard, hoping it was not the little dog from next door, digging in her flower garden again. The third time she heard the sound, she realized it was her niece.

Asia was moaning. Her soft moan erupted into a loud cry. "My baby... my baby... they killed my baby... they killed my baby!"

Pearl kneeled at the tub and rubbed Asia's shoulders. "Honey, you have to pull through this."

"Aunt Pearl, how could God have let this happen to my sweet baby?"

"I wish I could give you an answer and tell you there was a good reason for this; but there is none. It rains on the just and unjust," Pearl said as she wiped tears from Asia's face. "Sweetheart, you have to keep Eric's memory alive in your heart, and now is not the time to give up. God didn't do this, and you'll need your faith more than ever to survive." Pearl cupped her hand under Asia's face. "We love you, and we loved Eric. We'll help you get through this."

Asia laid her head on the side of the tub and cried.

"Let it out my sweet child. Let it all out."

The next morning, Asia entered the kitchen and saw her aunt and uncle at the table drinking coffee. She almost asked them where Eric was before the pain of reality hit her.

"How are you, precious? Sit and have a cup of coffee." Mike pulled out a chair for her.

"I want a private funeral for Eric. Just the family and close friends. I don't want a bunch of people who didn't even know my baby, touching him, staring at him." Asia sobbed.

Pearl embraced her niece. "Believe me, I understand your feelings, but Eric's death is a tragedy for everyone in this community. He's in heaven, funerals are for the living," Pearl said as she hugged Asia. "It's a way to show honor, and no one deserves honor more than Eric."

"The arrangements are made with "Riley Funeral Home, but we can change them if you want." Mike took a sip of his coffee before he continued to talk to Asia. "I know Mr. Riley, the owner of the funeral service, and he won't put up with a bunch of nonsense."

"Will my father be there, Uncle Mike?"

"Yes, I called him, and he said he'd come."

"Is Aunt Brenda going to be with him?"

"Don't know, honey. Why'd you ask me that question?" Mike and Pearl exchanged glances.

"I know about Dad and Aunt Brenda. I've known about them for a long time," Asia said as she remembered that awful day she heard her father and aunt in her mother's bedroom.

CHAPTER 6

Eric's funeral was surreal for Asia, she felt as if it was happening to someone else. Uncle Mike kept his word about not allowing any drama. Riley escorted anyone who acted out, into the foyer of the church. The media and their cameras had to stay outside. Local political leaders attended, but none gave speeches.

There were condolences from several other churches, and organization in the community. Joe, who was still in the hospital recovering from surgery, had his son send a note. It was standing room only in the packed church, and so many flowers that Asia wondered if the money should have gone to charity.

Harry came with his mother; she stood at Eric's casket weeping. Asia wanted to scream her crying over Eric now meant nothing.

Walter came into his grandson's funeral late and alone.

"Glad you could make it. Where's Brenda?" Mike whispered.

"Sorry, I don't know where she is?" Asia's father attempted to squeeze in beside her, but Mike would not slide over and Walter had to sit at the end of the row.

Asia wondered where Aunt Brenda was, but did not dwell on the subject. She focused on holding it together and breathing. *God help me make it one more day*, she prayed.

***

Walter sat at his grandson's funeral thinking he might have a special reserved place in hell for sleeping with the twin sister of his child's dying mother. He hoped Asia did not find out about him and her aunt. Mike told him and Brenda to get out and not come back; but Walter knew that was grief. He did not come back to see his child because of guilt, not because Mike banned him.

It had been thirteen years since he seen his daughter. Asia sat there in her time of need with her head on her uncle's shoulder and not his. Walter tried to call her a thousand times, but felt guilty. He would walk pass Mike's house, and try to find the courage to knock on the door.

It was better he stayed away he consoled himself. His life with her Aunt Brenda had been full of drama, and it was best his beautiful daughter missed exposure to their mess.

Linda and Brenda were different as night and day. Asia's mother was kind, quiet, and caring. Walter knew she loved him, Asia, and her family.

He was sure Brenda cared for herself, and realized too late that the qualities that attracted him to Linda's identical twin sister where the same ones that made him regret that decision.

Brenda was daring, exciting, and loved to party. She believed in living for today, but she did not believe in any sacrifices for herself or working hard to get what she wanted in life. As a result, they did not have much for long. Cars, apartments, jewelry, clothes, and good times came and went. They lost their last apartment in an upscale development and were now living with Walter's older brother four blocks away from Mike and Pearl.

Walter sat thinking about the scene he had with Brenda before coming to Eric's funeral. He entered the bedroom they shared in his brother's house. "Why aren't you getting dressed for the funeral," he asked her sitting on the side of the bed in a nightgown.

"Hell no, I ain't seen them in thirteen years. What I look like showing up now."

"Come-on Brenda, it's a rough time for Asia. We need to show her support. Plus Mike called, he must want us there."

"Oh, so now he calls. He could've called long time ago."

"He didn't know where we lived or the phone number. It's not as if we stayed still."

"I guess that's my fault...huh. How'd he know how to find us now?"

31

"My brother's wife saw Pearl at the market and told her we lived here."

"She has a big mouth. That's why I can't stay here."

"We don't have a choice unless you want to get a job."

Brenda screamed and pointed her finger, "I should've never hooked up with your poor ass." Walter slammed the door in her face and left to go to his grandson's funeral.

CHAPTER 7

Patty waived as she saw Asia approaching with her cleaning cart. A young boy darted around Patty and charged toward Asia with a woman running after him. The boy looked so much like Eric it caught Patty off guard. Asia stood still and gasped as the child ran past her. She tightened her grip on the cleaning cart, and her eyes filled with tears.

Patty screamed for Jay as she ran toward her friend. "Honey, are you okay?" she asked.

Asia did not respond and stood there with a blank expression on her face.

"What's going on?" Jay said running out of the office.

"It's Asia, help me with her."

Together, they pried Asia's hands from the cart and led her into the office where they placed her on the sofa. Jay put a cool cloth on Asia's forehead while Patty knelt next to her.

"Are you all right?" There was no answer and Patty turned to Jay, "Can you stay with her until I get back? I have to report to court."

"Sure, she'll be fine. Don't worry, go on I know how crazy the judge acts if you show up late."

Jay sat beside Asia and took her hand. "Do you want me to call your uncle?"

"No, Asia took a deep breath. "I can't call him every time I see a boy that reminds me of Eric. I feel so silly."

"Don't beat up on yourself. It's only been two months. Most people in your situation wouldn't be able to function. I can relate to what you're facing." Jay left the sofa, walked to the window, and looked through the blinds.

"It was difficult for me when Kiki's father, Keith, died in a car accident before our child was born. It took a long time for me to get over it; and after over five years, I still have bad days. Have you thought about grief counseling? I could go with you."

"Thanks Jay. I went once with Aunt Pearl, but it's not for me. I have to find my own way."

"I'm here if you ever need me."

***

Patty was in court longer than she expected. She hated it when lawyers asked the same dumb question in several different ways, hoping to get a different answer from the witness. Asia had gone by the time Patty returned. The trash bucket was empty, and her office was clean, but Jay was still at work.

"Why are you here?"

"I had some work I wanted to finish before I left today."

"Jay, it could've waited until tomorrow. What happened with Asia? She cleaned my office."

"I offered to call her uncle, but she said no."

"Her reaction to that little boy was painful. Who brings a small child to court?"

"Guess the child's guardian had no choice."

Patty frowned. "No choice, would you bring Kiki to the courthouse? There's nothing here a child needs to see."

"It's better than the cemetery where she often goes with me," Jay answered, hovering over her paperwork before she looked at Patty.

"Thank you, Jay," Patty nodded. I needed a jolt of reality. It's late, go home to your daughter. I'll see you tomorrow."

Patty walked into her office and closed the door. She thought about what Jay said, and how when she was a child, her grandmother took her everywhere. Grandmother Raizel did not believe in babysitters.

She sat in her chair and buried her head in her hands. Patty felt sad and exhausted. For the first time since Eric's death, she cried. Her whole focus had been on getting his killers, but she never took time to grieve for the child.

Today was confirmation that Asia needed help. The light had gone out of her friend's eyes, and it broke Patty's heart to see her that way. Eleanor, now Eric, she thought between sniffles.

Joyce A. Smith

Patty dried her eyes and called Eleanor's husband. "Hello Winston, how are you and the kids?"

"We're hanging in there."

"Winston, it's been eight months. Have you found a suitable person to take care of the kids?"

"I had someone. She was good and had the right credentials, but Lizzie cried every time the woman looked at her. I'm at my wits end, and I don't know what to do."

"There may be someone I know who would be perfect to take care of them," Pattie said as she thought of Winston's children, Lizzie and Win. Lizzie was the youngest, and she reminded Patty of Eleanor. The son resembled Winston.

"Really?"

"Yes, she's a good friend of mine. She lost her little boy in a shooting about two months ago. A change in scenery could be perfect for her, and I bet the kids would love her."

"I heard about that case on the news, and I think you told me about it, but didn't it happen in the inner-city of Baltimore?"

"Yes." Patty answered, irritated by Winston's question.

"Does she have a degree or training in child care?"

"No, she has a high school education, but is the kindest person I've ever met."

"For God sakes," Winston yelled. "You're suggesting I let a high-school educated, inner-city woman, who just lost her son to street violence, take care of my children. What in the world is wrong with you?"

Patty irritated and surprised at Winston's comments, stood from her chair and fired back. "Eleanor was my best friend, and Lizzie is my godchild." She banged her fist on the desk, "I love both of your kids as if they were my own. I'd only bring someone I could stake my life on to take care of your children. Winston sometimes you can be a real asshole!"

"I'm sorry, Patty," he responded in a low tone. "This has been difficult. Lizzie cries all the time, my son is overprotective of his sister, and he looks so sad. Win won't let Lizzie out of his sight. The boy is only seven and is sometimes more of a father to her than I am."

"It's been tough," Patty said, softening her voice. "Lizzie turned four right before Eleanor died. She doesn't remember when her mother was well. I haven't talked to my friend yet."

Patty sat and leaned back in her chair. "Why don't you and the kids meet her? I'll tell her we're coming to visit, and you can decide then. We'll come up next weekend."

"It can't hurt to meet her. I'll see you soon."

***

Winston hung up the phone feeling ashamed for speaking about Patty's friend in such a harsh manner. He closed his eyes, picked up the picture of his wife from his desk, and put it to his chest, "I'm messing up Eleanor, and saying

37

mean things to our friend. Our children are in pain---what should I do?"

Eleanor had been the strong one in their marriage. She was full of life, and he sat there holding her picture thinking how unfair it was she died. He distressed over the statements he made to Patty, and remembered how Eleanor often said when something happened in a low-income area, the media always found the person with the fewest teeth and lowest intelligence to interview. Her saying was, "The perception of the truth was always more compelling than the actual truth."

Winston enrolled Eleanor during the two years of her illness into two clinical trials for cancer treatment. Each time she appeared to get better, but after a while, the cancer would come back. Eleanor refused the third time he arranged another trial. She told him she was tired, but he could not believe she would not try again, and ignored how weak and fragile she had become. He wanted to hold on to her, and instead of being a comfort, spent her last days attempting to convince her to try one more time.

He came home from work a week before his wife died and found her reading the Bible. As Winston entered her room, she looked up at him and said, "I have fought the good fight." He could not believe she was quoting to him from the Bible.

The day Eleanor died; Winston sat beside his wife and felt her hand go limp as she took her last breath. He sat there childlike hoping if he held her hand long enough the heat from his hand would radiate to hers and bring his wife back to life. Winston's sister-in-law, Vivian, and his children, Lizzie, and Win were on the other side of the bed as Eleanor closed her eyes.

"Wake her up, Daddy," Win screamed at his father with tears covering his face. "Wake her up---please!"

His child's cry made Winston understand his wife had tried to get him to face reality and grasped he did his children a terrible injustice by not preparing them for their mother's death. Something he would have to endure.

CHAPTER 8

The young prosecutor left her office, thinking about the disturbing phone call she had with Winston. She was not only surprised, but also hurt he judged Asia without knowing her. It was out of character for him, and Patty hoped his upsetting behavior resulted from the frustration of not being able to find a suitable person to care for his children. Patty decided she would stop at Asia's house instead of going straight home from work.

Pearl greeted her at the door. "I'm glad to see you. Asia's in the living room."

The house still had an empty feeling. Patty walked into the living room and observed her friend sitting on the couch looking at old photos.

"I miss my mother," Asia said looking at the pictures in her lap. "Maybe if she were alive this wouldn't be so difficult. I should've been able to protect Eric."

"How? No one could have predicted what happened."

"I don't know, I felt something when I saw that guy walk toward the barbershop." Asia wiped a tear from her face. "If I had paid a little more attention, maybe Eric would not have died. Harry blames me for our child's death and says I'm stupid."

"If he wants to blame someone, he should blame himself because he was not a good father to Eric." Patty sat on the sofa and gently took Asia's hand. "There's nothing you could've done to stop this awful thing from happening."

Patty patted Asia's hand, looked into her friend's eyes, and asked, "I'm curious...what attracted you to Harry?"

Asia laid the photos of her mother on the coffee table and left the sofa. She walked to the front window and kept her back to Patty as she explained in a low voice. "Harry was different when I first met him. He was so sweet and kind with a toothpaste commercial smile and told me I was pretty. I'd never heard that from any man other than Uncle Mike, and I figured he only said it because we look alike."

"Yeah, funny how those family genes are, you look like your uncle right down to skin coloring and those hazel eyes you both have, but Asia, you have a mirror. You should've known how pretty you are."

Asia turned from the window, and faced Patty, "As stupid as it may sound, I thought we'd get married. After I became pregnant, I rarely saw Harry." Asia returned to the window. "I guess I'm similar to my mother, in choosing the wrong man." Asia sighed, "When you walk into a room Patty, you command attention and respect. You're smart, gorgeous, and strong. I'm not."

"Strength comes in many different forms. Sometimes a whisper is stronger than a scream. You're magnificent and special, if only you knew it."

Patty left the sofa and joined Asia at the window. She watched several children playing. "I want to share some information with you I haven't shared with many people. The main reason I wanted to be a prosecutor was as you know my mother died when I was ten years old, but you don't know how."

She stopped watching the kids and gave Asia her full attention. "My mother was a beautiful woman, and my father was always jealous of her. They were arguing and in a drunken rage, he pushed her so hard she fell and hit her head on the edge of the piano he and I used to play. She was in a coma for three days before she died. That's why it's so important that victims get justice."

"I'm sorry Patty."

"It was a long time ago." Patty took Asia's hand, "Let's go on a road trip to Boston. It will do us both good to get out of the city. I want you to meet my friend, Winston, and his kids."

"Isn't that Eleanor's husband?"

Patty nodded.

"Is he a doctor?"

"He's a research scientist. He tried to find a cure for his wife, but ran out of time."

Asia walked to the mantel over the fireplace, picked up a picture of her son, and ran her fingers around the frame. "The day my son was born, I held him in my arms and looked into his beautiful face. It was a great feeling knowing I was holding a real miracle. I don't know how I will ever get through this without him." She returned Eric's picture to the mantel. "Can't imagine how your friend manages. It must be difficult for him to raise his kids alone."

"Yes, but they're coping. Eleanor's death affected many people. It was challenging to watch her fight so hard for her life and lose." Patty felt herself tearing; the last thing she wanted to do was get emotional in front of Asia and cleared her throat. "Eleanor was my mentor, and she believed in me. I wouldn't be where I am today if it hadn't been for her."

"Why's that?"

"She was one of my undergrad professors. I was a poor girl from Louisiana on scholarship, and she took an interest in me. There were two important people in my life, Eleanor and my grandmother. Now they're both gone," Patty said as she averted her eyes.

Asia smiled, "Well, there're lots of other people who love you."

Patty smiled back. "So are you up to going on a trip with me?"

"I'm not sure I should leave Uncle Mike and Aunt Pearl. It's only been two months..."

"We'll be gone for a weekend. I'm sure they'll be all right. PLEASE---I hate driving to Boston by myself."

Joyce A. Smith

"I'll go, but only for the weekend. Where in Boston do they live?"

"Winston has a place in the city, but his father left him a home in Martha's Vineyard. They stay there every summer."

"Wow, I can't imagine having two homes." Asia returned to the sofa, picked up the photos of her mother from the coffee table, and placed them to her chest. "If it weren't for my Uncle Mike, we wouldn't have a home."

"Winston's family has money. They're not rich, but comfortable. Winston's father, Winston Churchill Augustus Sr., was surgeon before he died. Who knows what Winston's son, Winston Churchill Augustus, III, will be when he becomes a man."

"I didn't realize his son was a third. I always hear you call him Win."

"Well, I hope it stops with Win. A Winston Churchill Augustus IV would be entirely too much. It sounds like kings and barons," Patty said shaking her head.

"It's cool, reminds me of a rich heritage."

"You'd say that." Patty laughed. "See if you can get off this Friday. We'll leave early in the morning, take a leisure drive up there, and catch the ferry before rush hour."

"I guess it'll be okay. Uncle Mike and Aunt Pearl should be fine for a weekend."

"They'll be glad you're getting out of the house."

"Yeah, I hope I'll be good company."

"Don't worry. You will be."

During the short drive home, Patty drifted into memories of her parents. Once she arrived at home, Patty pulled out her family album and looked at her mother's photograph.

She was around the same age now that her mother was in the picture. They had the same slender build, texture of hair, and shade of light brown-skin coloring. If it were not obvious it was an old picture, she might think she was looking at herself---they could be twins.

Patty remembered her mother as gentle and carefree; she spoiled Patty. Grandmother Raizel also loved Patty but balanced her love. Her grandmother taught her how to be independent, strong, and confident, and to depend on no one but herself.

Grandmother Raizel never forgave Patty's father for killing her daughter and did not allow Patty to see him during his incarceration. Years after her grandmother's death, Patty found a stack of letters from her father, asking for forgiveness. She considered contacting him. *It's time to heal and forgive,* she thought running her finger over her mother's photograph.

CHAPTER 9

Asia was quiet as she prepared to meet Patty and tried not to disturb her aunt and uncle. She thought it was a joke when Patty told her what time they would leave; but Patty arrived at the designated time.

"It's still dark. Why do we have to leave so early?" Asia asked as she greeted Patty at the door.

"We want to get on the other side of New York before the traffic gets crazy."

"Okay, let me write a note for Aunt Pearl and Uncle Mike to tell them I'm gone."

"Come on, let's get going."

Exasperated, Asia glanced at her friend and exhaled. "Why are we in a hurry? I've gone to New York with Uncle Mike and Aunt Pearl many times, and we never left this early."

"Trust me; you'll be happy we left so early. We want to be at the Woods Hole ferry at least forty-five minutes before loading."

Asia had second thoughts about agreeing to go on this trip with Patty. She was not sure she was ready to meet new people so soon after Eric's death; she could not back out now.

The two friends arrived at the ferry early. Asia stood at the rail and looked out into the open water. The wind blew against her face as she listened to the water hitting the side of the ferry with a beat of its own. She thought how Eric would have loved riding the ferry. She felt the familiar pain threatening to tear out her heart. Asia fought hard to breathe and keep her eyes from tearing. *God please help me endure this pain*, she silently prayed.

"It won't be long before we reach the island." Patty said standing at the rail beside her. "When we get there, I'll drive you around. The island is so beautiful."

"What sort of man is Winston?"

"He's a good man, and he loved Eleanor. They were complete opposites." Patty turned and faced Asia as she continued. "Eleanor was outgoing while Winston is reserved. He can be guarded until he knows you."

"Will it be hard to talk to him?"

"No, but he doesn't make new friends as easily as Eleanor did. The only recent person Winston has met is a man named Glenn Peck. He met Glenn at a grief counseling session."

"That's great; he talks to someone who can relate."

"I guess, but I don't like Glenn. He reminds me of a buzzard waiting for a carcass."

"Wow, Patty; why not tell me how you really feel about this guy?"

Joyce A. Smith

"You might think I'm being rough, there's something fishy with him. I've never felt this way about anyone. Don't know what it is." She said shaking her head. "Glenn has met Winston at a vulnerable time, and I bet Eleanor wouldn't have liked Winston's new friend as she was good at reading people."

"I trust your instincts. If you say there's something's wrong, I believe you."

"Thanks Asia, but enough about Glenn. The house on the island belonged to Winston's father. It's a Victorian-style, built sometime in the sixties or seventies. Eleanor removed walls and gave the home an updated modern touch." Patty chuckled, "Winston refused to part with most of the furnishings in the house so nothing matches, but somehow Eleanor made it work."

"She had a unique sense of style, huh?"

"Good thing."

During the drive to Winston's house, Asia admired the elegant and massive homes in the area. "This island is beautiful, and the homes are huge. I'm a little nervous meeting your friend," she acknowledged feeling out of place.

"Let me tell you something, you have no reason to be nervous. Winston's regular."

"Yeah, but his status... and he owns two houses and...."

"Remember, it's easy to be successful when you've had a major head start. The real test of success is when you start with nothing."

"Like you, Patty?"

"What are you, my number one fan?"

"Yes, and don't forget it," Asia said smiling.

"We're at Winston's house," Patty stated as she pulled into his driveway and parked her car.

"Wow! It's gorgeous." Asia eyes shifted from the lush green landscape to the three-story mansion. "Looks similar to something I'd see on TV. Does he have a team of people to take care of the lawn and trees?"

"Remember, Winston inherited this house," Patty answered as they climbed out of the car and walked up the path to the front door.

Patty rang the doorbell, and a tall, slender man greeted them. Asia watched as Winston threw his arms around Patty with great excitement. He reminded Asia of a drowning man reaching for a life preserver. He was handsome and had the bluest eyes she had ever seen. His blond hair was receding; and she could not help but wonder if his hair loss was due to heredity or the stress of caring for his wife for the last two years of her life. The sharp pain in Asia's chest returned and made it hard for her to breathe. She wondered if the pain she felt was slow death from a broken heart.

"Winston, please meet Asia," Patty said after he released her. "Asia, Winston."

"It's very nice to meet you, Mr. Augustus."

"Call me Winston. Both of you please come in, we'll sit on the patio. It's nice out there this time of day."

"How was the ride up?" he asked.

"Not bad, we missed most of the traffic by leaving early."

Asia smiled, "She should say by leaving while it was still dark."

"That's my Patty, she doesn't mess round," Winston said smiling back at Asia.

"Where the kids?" Patty inquired.

"Vivian took them to the movies. They should be here any moment."

"How's Vivian? I haven't seen her since the funeral."

"She misses her sister, and she tries to spend time with the kids, more so with Lizzie." The sound of children running through the house interrupted Winston.

"Is Aunt Patty here yet?" Win called out as soon as he entered the house. Seconds later, he ran out onto the patio and into Patty's open arms.

"Hi Aunt Patty." he shouted.

Patty gave Win a bear hug and kissed him on the forehead.

"Hi there, little one," Patty said to Lizzie entering the patio as she gave the child a big hug and a kiss on the cheek.

"I'm glad you're here auntie."

"So am I."

"Hi Patty, it's good to see you," said Vivian, a well-dressed blonde-haired woman entering the patio after Lizzie and Win.

"Hi, Vivian, meet my friend Asia."

Vivian walked over and extended her hand to Patty's friend. "It is nice to meet you."

"It's nice to meet you, too."

Lizzie gave Asia a quizzical look, "You're real brown, like my brown crayons."

"Elizabeth," Winston shouted. Win rolled his eyes, Patty giggled, and Vivian stared straight ahead.

Tears flowed hard enough to wash away Lizzie's numerous red freckles.

"I'm so sorry." Winston apologized.

Asia threw her head back and laughed. It was the first time since Eric's death she laughed about anything. It felt so strange but good. "Yes I'm brown, Lizzie. Your crayons and people come in different shades. What a joy you are."

She wondered how many people of color the child had met, but before she judged, Asia remembered Eric had not met many white people. Patty may be one of the few black people the child knew, and Patty was fair. Uncle Mike said he thought Patty had Creole in her blood.

Asia stooped to Lizzie's level and touched her chin. "I bet you are not only pretty but smart."

Lizzie stopped crying, sniffed, and giggled. "I can count to one hundred, and I know my ABCs. Do you want to hear me?" she asked clapping her hands.

Asia saw the confused look on Winston's face when Lizzie giggled; and wondered why?

"Not now Lizzie," Winston interrupted.

"Maybe later," Asia said as she smiled at Lizzie, thinking how much she missed that childhood innocence.

"My brown and black crayons are my favorite because they are strong. Are you strong?" Lizzie asked Asia.

"Win and Lizzie, please go upstairs and let the adults catch up." Vivian instructed before Asia could respond. Lizzie crossed her arms and stomped her feet, "Why can't I catch up with Aunt Patty?"

"Not now," Winston replied in a sharp tone.

51

Win grabbed his sister's hand and led her out of the room. "Come on Lizzie. We'll talk to you later at dinner, Aunt Patty."

Lizzie turned back. "See you in a little while, Aunt Patty. See you Miss Asia."

Winston smiled and directed his attention to Asia. "I see my daughter's taken with you. It is rare for her to respond so well to someone she has just met."

"She's sweet." Asia thought about her brief conversation with the child who had compared her complexion to a brown crayon, and then she equated brown and black colors to strength. Asia shook her head. *Out of the mouths of babes,* her mother used to say.

Winston explained. "Although Lizzie's four, she still doesn't understand the differences in races."

Asia nodded. "Don't rush her. Let her keep her innocence. That knowledge will come soon enough. Right now should be a time of wonder for Lizzie."

"I'm sorry to hear about your little boy," Winston said stumbling over his words. "Patty told us how wonderful he was."

"Yes, he was a very special and precious gift," Asia said in a low voice and looked at her hands folded in her lap.

"What movie did you take the kids to see?" Patty asked Vivian.

Winston shot Patty a look and nodded.

"I took them to see *A Little Princess.*"

"Bet Win enjoyed that," Patty rolled her eyes.

Vivian chuckled. "You know Win. As long as Lizzie is happy, he does not care."

"Hope you like Italian, Asia," said Winston. "I've ordered an early dinner. I thought you two might be hungry after your trip. It should be here soon."

"Italian's fine."

Winston looked at Vivian and asked, "Do you mind entertaining Asia for a while? Patty and I have business we need to discuss in my study. I hope you don't mind Asia?"

"No, it's okay."

Vivian nodded at him. "Take your time. Asia and I will be just fine."

Asia wondered what she could talk about with Vivian. Patty told her Winston was down to earth, but could that extend to his sister-in-law? Vivian was one of those people Uncle Mike would say the world was their oyster. Asia never knew until now what that meant. Vivian surely appeared secure in her place in the universe and carried an air of prominence.

***

Patty turned to Winston as they entered the house with a big smile on her face, "You like her don't you?"

"Wait a minute Patty," Winston said as he closed the door behind them. He turned to her with a serious look on his face. "She's not what I expected. How old is she?" he asked as they proceeded to his study.

"She's two years younger than me, twenty-five."

"Asia looks younger, but she acts older."

"My friend has been through a lot in twenty-five years. Losing her son would be enough, but she also lost her mother to lupus when she was around twelve or thirteen. Her uncle and aunt raised her."

"I have to admit Lizzie seems to like her, but Asia would have to go back to school if she were to take the job."

"I'm sure that shouldn't be a problem, but the real question is how would you deal with her?"

"What you mean?"

"Come on Winston, you're talking to me. I saw the way you looked at her."

"I'm thirty-seven-years old. She's a child by comparison."

"Eleanor was younger than you."

"It wasn't that much difference in our ages, plus Eleanor had an advanced degree and had travelled the world."

"So, is this a class thing?"

"No Patty, this is she's young and has lost her child to violence thing!"

"You're right, and I'm out of line." Patty took Winston's hand. "I'm reacting to some of the comments you made about Asia."

"Sorry, that's not me. Sometimes I don't know what I'm saying, and when it comes to Lizzie, I have no idea what I'm doing. I really need help." Winston's voice cracked.

"It's been tough, but it'll get better. We're having this conversation, and you haven't even offered Asia the job."

"I have to convince her." Winston said slouched back in his chair. "Lizzie giggling was a rare treat," he said as he grasped Patty's hand.

Winston could not admit it to Patty, but her friend affected him in ways other than making his daughter happy. Asia was soft, willowy, and pretty. Looking at her smooth deep brown face with her enchanting hazel eyes made his heart beat faster. Winston surprised himself, he felt giddy as a teenager.

"I know it was my idea to bring Asia here, but it will not be easy to get her to leave her aunt and uncle." Patty offered cutting into Winston's thoughts. "It will be difficult, she's devoted to them, and they're devoted to her."

CHAPTER 10

Vivian was distant, but polite after Winston and Patty left. She asked Asia where she lived and worked and nodded her head after receiving the information. Their conversation was awkward, and Asia was relieved when they reentered the patio.

"I hope we weren't away too long," Winston said as he sat next to Asia.

"Not at all," Vivian answered. "Asia and I had a wonderful conversation."

Patty suggested places to visit on the island. Winston also offered a few suggestions while Vivian made no comments.

Winston admonished Lizzie at dinner for talking with her mouth full. Patty told Asia how difficult it had been for Winston because of Lizzie to keep someone to take care of the kids. Asia wondered if he was choosing the wrong people, Lizzie was an engaging, lovable child. Win was the one that deserved concern. He was much too serious for a young boy, and she did not see him once take his steel-blue eyes off

Lizzie. Win reminded Asia of a ninja robot---ready to defend his sister at all costs.

"Daddy, I want to show Miss Asia my room," Lizzie said after placing her fork on her plate.

"Miss Asia just finished eating dinner. Plus, she's Daddy's company, not yours."

Lizzie crossed her arms and pouted.

"I don't mind Mr. Augustus, if it's okay with you?" Asia said as she placed her napkin next to her plate.

"Remember, it's Winston, are you sure?"

"Come and go with us, Win," Lizzie pleaded with her brother, before Asia could answer.

Lizzie and Win guided Asia out of the dining room, and towards the staircase. As Asia walked through the house, she admired the artwork, the paintings on the walls, and the sculptures were amazing. The only piece of art she owned was a sculpture Patty had given her.

Asia spotted vases and lamps etched with Victorian-looking women; paired with abstract paintings. She understood exactly what Patty meant about Eleanor decorating the home with a mixture of modern and traditional furniture and artwork. Asia loved her home, but this house was magnificent. She wondered how Winston's regular home in Boston looked if this was the summerhouse.

"Close the door, Win," Lizzie insisted as they entered her bedroom.

Asia's mouth parted as she looked around Lizzie's room. It resembled a large playroom for several children, with a dollhouse; and shelves full of dolls, books, and huge stuffed animals in each corner.

"We heard Daddy say something about your little boy." Lizzie said while playing with one of her dolls.

Asia frowned. "How did you hear your father say that?"

"We were by the patio door," Lizzie admitted.

"I told her to come on." Win answered.

"You did not."

"I did too."

"You both know it's not nice to eavesdrop on adults."

"We know," Win replied.

"What happened to your son?" Lizzie asked undeterred.

"He...went...to...heaven," Asia stumbled.

"My Mommy went to heaven. She could take care of your little boy, and then you won't have to be sad anymore. What's his name?"

"Eric."

"Get on your knees, Miss Asia. Win, kneel with us."

They did as Lizzie instructed, she clasped her hands and prayed. "Dear Lord, please ask my mommy to take care of Eric. Amen."

"Amen," said Asia and Win.

Lizzie asked Asia to read her favorite book to her and Win. Asia sat in the rocking chair in the room and read.

***

"I have never seen Lizzie react to a person she didn't know well as she has to Asia," Vivian commented as they continued to sit at the dining room table.

Winston nodded. "You're right, and since we're on the subject, I'm considering offering Asia a job taking care of the kids."

"What! Does she have training in the child-care field? What is her educational level? I didn't get the feeling she had any degrees or training that would qualify her enough to take care of your children." Vivian looked at Patty with wide eyes. "I think she is a nice person and I agree that Lizzie seems to like her, but that is not enough to have her raise my niece and nephew."

"What are you saying, Vivian? Asia didn't walk in here splitting verbs and pronouns. She may not have a degree, but she's not ignorant. There's no need to worry; she won't have the kids speaking slang or broken English."

"Don't say that Patty! I'm not attacking her, but what qualifies her to take care of Lizzie and Win?"

Winston cut in, "I don't think Vivian meant any..."

"Stay out of this!" Patty cut him off in mid-sentence. "This is between us."

Vivian faced Patty with anger in her eyes. "I know how close you and Eleanor were, and how much you love Lizzie and Win, but those kids are my blood." Her voice quivered, "I have every right to be concerned regarding their welfare."

"Where's your concern when Lizzie's crying at night for her mother? I know you love them, but you don't live with them." Patty pointed her finger. "You reside in Vermont. Winston has hired four people in less than eight months. If Asia takes the job, she'll love these children. That's something you don't learn in a graduate program."

"She lost her little boy. She is dealing with her own grief. Is it even fair to ask her to take on this responsibility?"

"Maybe we should let Asia make that call." Patty said as she heard the kids and Asia coming downstairs. The kids made a detour to the TV in the next room.

Winston stood and approached Asia. "I see you're back from your great adventure with my daughter and son. Could I speak to you for a moment in my study?"

"Yes, Mr. Augustus. I mean Augustus. Would you mind if I called you Augustus instead of Winston? Augustus sounds like royalty." Asia smiled.

Winston let out a loud belly laugh. "Sure you can, but it may take more than my last name to make me royalty."

As he laughed, Vivian and Patty looked at each other, and then looked at Winston.

***

Asia saw a picture sitting on Winston's desk of a beautiful woman with red hair---*this must be Augustus' late wife, Eleanor.* Lizzie resembled a young version of this woman, red hair, and freckles included. Asia wondered if maybe Lizzie looking so similar to her mother was responsible for why Augustus had a hard time handling his child.

"I want to offer you a job," Winston said as they entered his study. "You have captured my child's heart. I've never seen Lizzie respond so well to anyone she has just met." Winston picked up Eleanor's picture and held it. "I want you to take care of her and Win, but you'd have to return to school, and I'll pay you to do that. You could go in the evenings, and weekends when I'm home from work, or you could do online classes." Winston returned Eleanor's picture to his desk and looked at Asia.

"Would I live here?"

"Yes, here in the summer and at my other house the rest of the time. In both houses, your room is not far from Lizzie and Winston's rooms."

"I appreciate your offer, but I have a job, and the only child I've ever taken care of was my son," she said as her voice strained. "I'm not sure that leaving my uncle and aunt so close after Eric . . ."

"I'm prepared to pay you more than you are making now plus free room and board, if you could give me a year or two, long enough to help Lizzie through this rough time in her life." Winston sat on the edge of his seat. "You've only been here a few hours, and it is the best time we've had since Eleanor passed. Lizzie is happy, smiling, and laughing when she is often whining and crying." Winston sat back in his chair. "I'm willing to meet your aunt and uncle. I know you've been through a tough time, but this could be a fresh start for you."

Asia looked into Winston's eyes and smiled, "All right, but I must warn you, my Uncle Mike will not be an easy sell."

***

Vivian twisted and turned in the bed, but could not sleep. She went downstairs to the kitchen and made herself a cup of tea. She took it to the dining room table, looked up from her tea, and saw Patty entering the room.

"I couldn't sleep," said Patty.

"Me either."

"I'm sorry about the conversation between us earlier." Patty said as she sat across the table from Vivian.

"I've been thinking of our discussion, and I have nothing against Asia." Vivian took a sip of her tea. "Maybe I am a little jealous?"

"What'd you mean, jealous?"

Vivian got up from the table, walked over to the window, and observed a full moon lightening the dark sky. "I met Winston first," she said turning from the window. "He was an intern working under my father and he would visit our home. He was always courteous, but I had hoped he would one day show me more. The hope ended when Winston met Eleanor," Vivian said turning back to the window.

"What happened?"

"Eleanor came home on spring break, and strolled into the parlor Winston and my father were sitting in reviewing a paper." Vivian sighed, "She looked like Jessica Rabbit. Her flowing red hair appeared to blow in the wind even though we were inside. Each freckle on her smooth and creamy face appeared to beckon to Winston."

"Did you see this as a second chance with Winston?"

Vivian returned from the window, sat and took another sip of her tea. "I don't know how I feel about him; so much time has passed. I remember how my heart sank when he first met Eleanor." Vivian looked across the table at Patty. "Today was déjà vu; Winston looked at Asia the same way he looked at Eleanor."

CHAPTER 11

On the ride home from Martha's Vineyard, Asia wondered how she should approach her aunt and uncle about taking the job in Boston. She laughed when she thought of how Patty's friend reacted when she called him Augustus.

"What are you laughing at?" Patty asked.

"Just thinking how shocked you and Vivian looked when Augustus laughed the other night."

"We haven't heard Winston laugh in a very long time, and you calling him Augustus was hysterical. Are you taking the job?"

"I'm leaning in that direction. It's a major decision."

"How'd you think Uncle Mike will react?"

"I'm not sure, but I won't take the job if he disapproves."

"Asia, I know you love your uncle, but it's your life and this should be your decision."

"Come to dinner tomorrow Patty and we'll talk to him together. You know Augustus, and if I decide to take the job, I'll need you and Aunt Pearl behind me if I have any chance with Uncle Mike."

Patty stopped a block from Asia's house at the red light in front of the neighborhood park. "I see its business as usual," she said pointing to a group of young men. "They don't even care about the darkness. They're huddled around the lights as if selling drugs is legal."

"I played baseball in this park as a young girl, and we'd make our own bases. I was the pitcher because I had a good arm."

"Those chicken wings," laughed Patty.

"Laugh all you want. I'd strike all the boys out, and they hated that."

"I bet they did."

"Seems a thousand years ago."

"I'll see you tomorrow," Patty said dropping Asia at her front door.

Asia was quiet as she entered the house; she did not want to disturb her aunt and uncle as she brought in her over-night bag and sat it in the hallway. She entered the living room, turned on the lamp, and reclined in Uncle Mike's favorite chair. Asia had considerable thinking to do and wanted to make the right decision about going to Boston. It sounded as if it was an opportunity for her, but she had never lived apart from her uncle and aunt.

She decided to put her fears aside and take Augustus' offer. This could be what she needed to rebuild her life, and she was glad she had asked Patty to come to dinner, and help her talk to her aunt and uncle. Asia approached her aunt the next morning and told her she had news to share.

"What is it Asia?"

"It's nothing bad but I need Uncle Mike in a real good mood. Do you mind preparing a nice dinner for tonight? I've invited Patty, I'll tell you then."

Pearl wrapped her arms around her niece, "Of course I don't."

It was the first big meal Asia's aunt had prepared since Eric's death, and she went all out. The golden fried chicken was delicious, and the macaroni and cheese was just the way Mike liked it with the top browned. Pearl's sweet potatoes with the pecan crust and green beans seasoned with smoked turkey necks helped set the stage.

Asia left the table after the main meal and retrieved the apple pie her aunt baked. She cut a big piece for her uncle and put vanilla ice cream on top. "Here you are Uncle Mike," she said as she handed him the plate with the pie and ice cream.

The mood was just right; her uncle had finished eating and had one of his favorite artists playing in the background. Asia found a Carmen McRae recording re-mastered onto a CD at a flea market and gave it to him. *It's now or never.* Asia nodded to Patty as a signal she was about to approach the subject.

"Uncle Mike and Aunt Pearl, I have a great opportunity that I want to share with you," Asia announced. "Winston Augustus, Patty's friend in Boston, offered me a job taking care of his two children. He will pay for college, and room and board is free. What do you two think?"

Mike banged his fist on the table. "Hell, no Asia! You will not live in a house with a man we don't know."

"Uncle Mike, I know Winston very well and I trust him with my life," added Patty.

"It's not your life," Mike returned.

"Not yours either," said Pearl. "I know you love Asia, but it's her decision."

"Pearl, Asia don't know how at one time, the only jobs black women could get were maids, cooks, or nannies. I won't allow her to do that!" Mike let out a deep sigh. "Plus, Boston is one of the most prejudice places in the world---she just as well be in Mississippi."

"Uncle Mike, things have changed. I'll be making much more than I am now, have a car available, and attend school. I work as a janitor. How much worse is this job? Plus, I have a connection with Augustus' little girl, Lizzie."

"That's not your child, Asia," Mike stated. "Don't try to substitute her for Eric and don't be taken in with the poor motherless child bullshit."

"Mike, that's enough." Pearl shouted.

"Look Asia," Mike walked around the kitchen table and put his hand on his niece's shoulder. "You're a grown woman and you must make your own decisions. I don't want you hurt. You've been through enough. I've a lot more experience in life than you have."

"Uncle Mike, you are a very good judge of character," said Patty. "Please meet Winston and judge for yourself. He's a wonderful man."

"Why I need to meet him?"

"Have an open mind, Mike," Pearl pleaded. "Please Mike, have an open mind."

***

Michael Wallace sat at the kitchen table alone after the women left the kitchen with his head in his hands. He had been through great trials in his life: segregation, Jim Crow, Vietnam, and the problems in his community; however, nothing could compare with losing Eric. It was an unspeakable pain, and he wondered if his own arrogance had contributed to Eric's death. His beloved neighborhood had been going downhill for a while. There had been other shootings, robberies, assaults, and murders. He did not believe it could happen to his family and had not thought about the danger he was putting them in by staying.

He purchased his house on Lafayette Avenue, twenty-five years ago with the GI Bill benefits. It was an open door for anyone that needed a place to stay, and several members of his family had lived here. Many stayed for months, others for years. This home served as a lighthouse in their storms and questioning himself for staying would not help.

No one in the family had seen Brenda. He told her to leave and not come back, but that was thirteen years ago. As long as he stayed, she could find him. He blamed himself for what happened to Eric. He should have gone to the barbershop with them. *I can't bring Eric back, but no one else will hurt Asia,* he vowed.

CHAPTER 12

It was not easy, but the three women convinced Mike to go to Boston. They also made him promise to be courteous when he met Winston. Mike did not complain when Patty showed up in the early hours of the morning to accompany them on the trip. Patty took precautions and called from the road to let Winston know they were on their way; she wanted to make sure the visit was smooth, with no surprises.

***

Winston was anxious about meeting Asia's aunt and uncle. He knew he had to make a good impression on her family if he wanted Asia to accept the position taking care of his children. An hour after Patty called, his friend, Glenn, showed up at his front door uninvited.

"Why are you here?" Mike asked opening the front door. "Asia and her family will be here soon."

"Relax, you told me they were coming, but I didn't realize it was today," Glenn said entering the foyer. "I saw your car in the driveway and wondered why you were in town."

Winston nodded and checked his watch.

"Where the kids?"

"They're with their aunt. Please Glenn, I don't want to be rude, but I'm meeting Asia and her family today," Winston repeated.

"It's not the Queen and the Royal family."

"This visit is important, and I don't want you ruining this for me." Winston remarked striking out at his friend.

"What do you mean I could ruin your meeting with Asia's family? Are you referring to my, as you call it, conservative views? I live in the real world, Winston."

"No matter what you call your ideas, I don't need you insulting Asia's family. According to Patty, Asia's uncle, has very strong opinions regarding race and politics."

"What you mean is he doesn't like white people." Glenn laughed.

"I wouldn't say that. He grew up in the height of the civil rights movement. His experiences are different from ours."

"Guess so, we're not black. He came up in a time when black people had to fight hard for dignity." Glenn flipped his hand, "Now they won't even keep their pants up around their waist."

"That's what I'm talking about," Winston barked. "I don't need this today, please leave!"

"I'm your friend and you're throwing me out of your house because of people you don't even know."

Winston apologized, realizing how little he knew about his friend. Other than his late wife, Glenn never talked of having any family or friends. Winston had heard his friend's political views, but did not know his hobbies, taste in music, or even what books he enjoyed. Most of their conversations centered on how Eleanor's death affected the children. It had not dawned on Winston until this very moment, how one sided their interactions were.

"I'll be on my very best behavior," Glenn said intruding into Winston's thoughts. "Besides, you look as if you could use some back-up," he added closing the front door.

"No I don't," Winston remarked as he walked towards his study. "Patty is coming with Asia and her family."

"Patty!" Glenn replied with clasped hands, "How wonderful."

Winston turned with a scowl to face his friend, Glenn's comment concerning Patty's visit hit a nerve. He knew Patty and Glenn did not like each other and neither of them made it a secret. He questioned if there was something about Glenn that Patty saw and wondered if Eleanor would have liked him. Winston never thought of these things until now. He hoped he was just nervous.

Several minutes later, the doorbell rang again. Winston stood still, realizing he should have gotten rid of Glenn. "That's the bell ringing," he said as an afterthought.

"Okay, mums the word," Glenn pretended to zip his mouth as he took a seat in Winston's study.

"Stay here. I'll be back."

Winston looked around the house and made sure Glenn was nowhere in sight before he opened the front door to his visitors.

"Hello, welcome." Winston said with a big smile.

He led them into an oblong-shaped room decorated with exquisite furnishings and a Steinway and Sons' black baby-grand piano. Across from the entrance was a fireplace with a marble mantle; and on both sides of the mantle were three columns of built-in shelves that housed numerous pieces of artwork, vases, bowls, crystals, and carvings from several places Winston and Eleanor had traveled in Asia, Africa, the Middle East, North America, and the Mediterranean,

"Please could I get anyone something to drink?" Winston offered.

Patty began making the introductions after everyone declined Winston's offer. "Winston, meet Asia's aunt and uncle, Pearl and Michael Wallace."

"Call us Mike and Pearl," Asia's aunt said as she extended her hand to Winston. At first Mike hesitated, but then also extended his hand.

"It's so nice to meet you," Winston replied. "Hello Asia."

"Hello Augustus." Asia smiled.

So far so good, Winston thought as he engaged Mike and Pearl in small talk. He asked questions about Baltimore, where they grew up, and what other cities they may have lived. He felt his nervousness leaving and hoped Glenn continued to stay in his study.

CHAPTER 13

Glenn entered the living room smiling. Patty looked at Winston and he looked at the floor.

"Hello everyone, my name is Glenn. I'm Winston's friend. Asia, I've heard so many good things about you, and I get to meet your family," he said extending his hand to her.

"It's a pleasure to meet you Glenn. This is my aunt and uncle, Pearl and Mike Wallace."

Glenn shook Pearl's hand first: *Oh my God! It's Aunt Pearl. She's heavier and has mixed grey hair; but I know it's her.* Thirty years had passed since Glenn seen his aunt, but he recognized her. He spent most of his childhood staring at her picture and dreaming she would come and rescue him. He had to compose himself and let her hand go. Patty and Winston were watching him with peculiar stares. Glenn wondered if his aunt recognized him since it had been so long and hoped she did not.

"Nice to meet you," Pearl smiled. "Have we met? You seem familiar."

Glenn shook his head in doubt. "I don't think so."

Pearl continued, "There's something about you, it could be your nice smile."

Glenn blushed before looking at the floor. Patty and Winston stared at each other as Glenn extended his hand to Pearl's husband and they exchanged greetings.

Mike appeared much larger when Glenn was a child. He did not have his afro and dashiki, was older, and had a head full of grey hair; but the boy now a man remembered him.

"It was a pleasure meeting everyone. Sorry I have to leave. Please have a great evening."

"Nice to meet you," Pearl said, as Asia and Mike nodded in agreement.

Patty approached Glenn as he turned to leave. "Wait, I'll walk you to the door."

"What was that?" Patty asked as they reached the front door. "You standing there holding Aunt Pearl's hand. We both know how you look down on anyone that is not part of your small world."

"You don't know anything about me. For your information, Winston asked me to be nice to Asia and her family," Glenn said lowering his voice. "That's what I was doing. Do you have a problem with me being nice? I know it's difficult for *you*."

"I can't believe you'd be nice just because Winston asked. You always have an agenda."

"Good night. I'm leaving before either of us says something we'll regret."

"Great idea Glenn, but I can't say anything to you I'd regret," Patty said as she closed the front door in Glenn's face.

"Winston how long, have you known your friend?" Pearl asked, as Patty returned to the living room.

"Not long. I met him at a grief counseling session eight months ago when my wife died. Why'd you ask Pearl?"

"He reminds me of someone I knew a long time ago."

"Pearl, don't start. It's not him," Mike said.

"Not who?" Asia asked as she turned to her aunt.

"No one," Pearl said as a tear moistened her face.

"Are you crying, Aunt Pearl?"

"You should tell them," said Mike.

Pearl dabbed at her tears. "Not now."

"Somebody, please tell me something." Asia inquired, looking from her aunt to her uncle.

Winston tapped Mike on the arm, "Maybe we should leave and let the women talk. Will you come with me to my study?"

"Yes, that sounds good."

***

Pearl let out a deep breath after the men left the room, "Winston's friend reminds me of someone I knew a long time ago...my nephew, Brian."

"Your nephew," Asia stumbled. "You never said you had a nephew named Brian."

Pearl clenched her hands to stop them from shaking. She explained in a low voice, "Brian was a boy the last time I saw him. This was before Mike and I got married; and way before you were born."

She took Asia's hand into hers. "Tonya, my baby sister, had a child when she was sixteen, and named him Brian. She'd never say who the father was, but it was obvious Brian's father was white." Pearl left the sofa, walked over to the mantle, and picked up one of the crystal bowls before continuing. "We went to the police, but Tonya cried every time we pushed her to tell us who the father was. After a while, everyone just stopped asking." Pearl continued to caress the bowl, "About the time Brian turned seven, I moved to Baltimore to be with Mike and get a job."

Pearl had fond memories of when she first met Mike. He had just gotten back from a tour in Vietnam and was visiting with her next-door neighbor. Her heart fluttered, as she saw him in his uniform, looking so proud and handsome with his chocolate skin coloring and beautiful hazel eyes. It was a difficult time for veterans returning from Vietnam, as they did not receive the same treatment as veterans from other wars. People demonstrated against the Vietnam war; and would sometimes spit on the service men. She fell hopelessly in love with Mike. Pearl smiled thinking how after all these years together, she was still hopelessly in love with him.

She returned the bowl to the mantle and turned to face Patty and Asia. "I told my sister once I got settled, I'd send for her and Brian. I'd been in Baltimore almost six months when I sent bus tickets for them to come live with me. Tonya was so excited and happy. I'd found a cute little apartment." Pearl chuckled, "I should call it a large room with a kitchenette, small bathroom, bed, and a pullout sofa. I knew Tonya and Brian would love it until we could do better."

"So what happened?" Asia asked.

"I received a call the night Tonya was to come to Baltimore from one of her neighbors, telling me Tonya had fallen down the steps at the church where she cleaned, and died. Tonya's neighbor saw Brian get into the Peck's car, but at the time didn't know my sister was dead." Pearl retrieved the bowl from the mantle. "By the time we arrived in South Carolina, the Pecks were long gone with my nephew. That's when we realized the pastor was Brian's father," Pearl sobbed.

"Aunt Pearl, why didn't you tell me about your nephew?" Asia put her arms around her aunt's shoulders.

"It was painful, and you were too young to be burdened with this information. After Linda died, you had your own situation."

"Did you say the pastor's last name was Peck?" Patty inquired. "That's Glenn's last name. What a coincidence, even though I don't believe in coincidences, and I find it hard to believe that Glenn could be your nephew, Aunt Pearl." Patty shook her head. "What makes you think you so?"

"Brian fell when he was a boy and cut his left eye. It left a scar similar to the one Glenn has over his left eye. Brian was born with an extra finger. The mid-wife tied a string around it and after a few weeks, the finger fell off, leaving a small bump on the side of his right hand. I felt a bump when he shook my hand."

Pearl got up from the sofa, returned the bowl to the mantle, walked over to the piano, hit three keys, and turned to face Patty and Asia before continuing. "Brian had a small gap in his front teeth, grey eyes that appeared to change colors, and he would look down when he talked. I noticed these same mannerisms in Winston's friend. I'd scold Brian about not looking at people when he talked to them."

She returned and sat on the sofa, "The only difference I can see between Brian and Glenn is Brian's hair was curlier and darker, but he was a boy then and people change."

Patty huffed, "Glenn looks down when he talks because everything coming out of his mouth is a lie. Many people have those same characteristics you described. Several years have passed, and you can't base an identification of someone on a boy you knew thirty years ago. If it was him why'd he pretend to be someone else, Aunt Pearl?"

"I wish I knew," Pearl put her head in her hands. "It makes no sense, but I feel in my gut it's him. I'm just not sure."

"It's not Brian. Trust and believe if it were, it's not the same little boy you remembered and loved."

***

Winston offered Mike a seat after the two men entered his study. Would you like a cocktail?"

"Yes, I'll take a little something on the rocks. Whatever you have is satisfactory. I have to keep my head clear; Pearl and me are driving to New York to stay with my brother when we leave here."

"You are more than welcome to stay. So, Asia and Patty won't have to ride the train home."

"Thanks, but my brother is expecting us, and he wouldn't take no for an answer."

"I don't know why meeting Glenn upset Pearl so much."

"It's a very long story. He reminds her of someone she once knew."

"Hope she'll be fine."

"Thank you. I'm sure she will."

Winston opened his credenza and pulled out the drawer that contained various bottles of alcohol, an ice bowl, and two glasses.

"Is cognac all right?"

"Yes, thank you."

Mike looked around Winston's study. It was tasteful and simple with several books stacked in the book selves that lined the room. He observed a picture on Winston's desk of Winston, a woman holding a baby, and a young boy. "Was this your wife? She was beautiful."

"Yes, thank you. The baby she's holding is our little girl, Lizzie, and the boy is our son, Win. The picture was taken before Eleanor became ill."

Winston walked over to the window. He stood there for a few seconds looking at the rain. "I appreciate you and Pearl coming to see me," he said as he turned and sat in a chair next to Mike. "I know how much Asia values you. She is a special person."

Asia's uncle nodded in agreement. "Yes, she is, and I think of her as my child. When my sister first brought her home from the hospital, I was very upset with my sister for becoming pregnant by a man I didn't care for and because she had lupus, but when I saw Asia, my heart melted as I held her in my arms. She was the most beautiful baby I'd ever seen."

Mike pulled out his wallet and showed Winston a picture of Asia's son. "Her little boy, Eric, was her world, and I don't know how she's able to function. This is a very difficult time for my niece. She's vulnerable, fragile, and, I don't want her trying to substitute your little girl for her son."

"He was a good-looking child," Winston said as he looked at Eric's picture. Returning the picture to Mike, Winston stood from his chair, and walked back to the window. The room was quiet except for the sound of rain hitting the window. Winston let out a sigh, and turned from the window to face Mike. "Eleanor was sick, on and off for two years. There were times we thought she was getting better, but then she'd become sick again." He resumed talking and sat beside Mike. "Eleanor died, when Lizzie was four and Win seven. My wife died three days after Lizzie's birthday. For most of my daughter's young life, her mother had been sick."

"That had to be really hard on both of your children."

"Asia is the first person outside of family that Lizzie connected to since my wife died. I took her to a child psychologist, and she sat and stared at the woman for several sessions. Mike, without a doubt Asia is exceptional. She's inviting, warm, disarming...."

"She is a young woman going through the most difficult time of her life, and I won't let anyone, and I seriously mean no one take advantage of her." Mike sat on the edge of his chair facing Winston. "I don't think coming here looking after your kids is good for her. She may be trying to run from her pain, and I'm not comfortable with her living with you. I don't know you."

"I understand how you feel, but taking care of my kids would be a good opportunity for Asia to start again. Staying where she is has to be a constant reminder of what happened," Winston said looking Asia's uncle in the eye. "How can she heal under those circumstances? I *promise* you I won't say or do anything, or let anyone around me give her grief; and I would never try to take advantage of her."

"I'm not happy about this." Mike takes a deep breath, "But I won't stand in her way if this is what she wants to do." Mike exhales and looks at the window. The rain has become heavy. "You might be right; a change could be what she needs to help her get through this horrible ordeal." Mike stands over Winston, still seated, "But at the first sign of trouble, I'll be back to get her, and this---*I promise*."

CHAPTER 14

Glenn's mind was on his Aunt Pearl as he drove from Winston's house to his home in Back Lake. Thirty years was a long time, but he remembered his aunt. He even recalled her scent. Pearl loved lavender soap, and after all those years, she still bathed with it.

He entered his house through the garage and could feel the heavy loneliness; the ticking of the clock on the mantel in the parlor was the only audible sound.

Glenn went upstairs to his bedroom and headed to the back of his walk-in closet where he pulled out a small sack containing a wooden box. He wondered why he kept the box in his closet when he had a safe downstairs in his study.

He had made the box composed of ice cream sticks when he was a child. He opened it and took out a black-and-white photograph of two young black women and a small pale boy with curly hair standing between them. The photo wrapped in an old piece of frayed cloth that had faded. Glenn handled it with care as he ran his fingers around the outlines of the two women and stared at himself as a child---his name then was Brian Adams.

"You are the only two people on this earth I ever loved, but my life is different now," he said as he looked at the photograph. *I have done things you could never understand. I'm not that little boy anymore.* Glenn walked over to the dresser and took a long look in the mirror. He kept his hair short, straightened, and dyed light brown. There was no trace of Brian left in his appearance, or his heart.

Glenn caressed the little box, remembering how long it took him and Blue, his only friend when he was young, to collect enough ice cream sticks to make it. They picked most of the sticks out of the trash after folks had eaten the ice cream and thrown the sticks away.

He and Blue were complete opposites but inseparable. Brian was a small child with gray eyes and fair complexion. The kids that lived around his home harassed him by calling him *Whitey.* His friend was big for his age, and so dark the kids called him *Blue.* Brian's friend could have beaten any child that called him by that name, but said the joke was on the name callers. Blue told Brian he liked the color blue because God made the sky blue.

Glenn knew his friend accepted the name-calling to make the young boy feel better. The day Brian and his mother were to catch the train to go live with Aunt Pearl was one of the most exciting days of Brian's young life. He hated leaving his friend, but figured life in Baltimore had to be better than it had been in Yellow Pond, South Carolina.

"I'll be right back," his mother told him. "I have to go to the church. Pastor Peck owes me money for cleaning, and we need every penny we can get." She bent over and kissed him on the cheek. "Your Aunt Pearl will take care of us until I get a job."

His mother never came back. Waiting for hours, Brian was hungry and afraid. He thought of walking to the church, but his mother told him to wait, he did not know what to do.

Hours later, Pastor Leonard Peck and his wife, Mary, pulled up in front of Brian's house. Peck told him to get his bag and get in the car.

"I'm waiting for my mother."

"She ain't coming. Get in the car," Peck said with a mean cold look on his face.

Brian stood still crying until Mary climbed out the car, walked over to him, and slapped him in the face.

"Get your white-looking ass in the car," she ordered, before grabbing him and pushing him in the back seat. "When we tell you to do something; you better do it. Just remember boy, you might look white, but you still just a nigger."

The child rode in the back of the car for hours, crying and wondering where his mother was. He was afraid, hungry, and had to go to the bathroom. Brian did know where he was or what time it was when Pastor Peck stopped and pulled into a rest stop, and took him to the bathroom.

"I'll tell you this one time, and never ask me again," Peck said to Brian. "Your mother's dead. She fell down the steps in the church." He grabbed the young boy by the arm. "You'll be living with my wife and me. If anyone asks you, you're my son. If you ever tell anyone anything different, I'll kill you. Then I'll find your Aunt Pearl and kill her too. Do you understand?"

Brian stood there looking up at the big burly white man with hard eyes and a mean mouth. The man resembled an evil villain in the stories his mother read to him, except those stories had happy-endings.

"Yes, sir," he sobbed with tears soaking his face.

"Stop that crying. From now on do as you're told."

Glenn stopped thinking about his childhood and put a Muddy Waters CD in his Bose player. Muddy had been his mother's favorite singer, and he felt lucky when he found a re-mastered copy. In his office at the bank, he played classical music. When he was home alone, he played the blues where he could be his mother's son, Brian Adams.

The pastor changed the boy's name to Glenn Peck, but did not change his name on the birth certificate, and used a fake christening certificate to make the new identity. Once Glenn found his birth certificate, he set up two social security numbers and identifications for himself, one in the name of Brian Adams, and the other as Glenn Peck. He made sure he never confused the two.

He wrapped the photo in the cloth, placed it back into the box, and returned the box to its hiding place. Afterwards, he sat on the side of the bed, and did something he had not done since he was seven-years old; Glenn cried.

***

The emotion of seeing Aunt Pearl caused Glenn to fall asleep in his clothes. He woke up thinking how she could be a problem for him. Glenn liked the life he now lived and had paid heavy dues. It was his time to reap the rewards, and he did not want Aunt Pearl or anyone interfering with his lifestyle. If she had found him thirty years ago, he thought, things might have been different; but now he had respectability, money, and power.

"Maybe she didn't recognize me," he said looking in the mirror. His gut was telling him his hope was *wishful thinking.* Glenn seldom planned his next moves. Most things in his life just happened, such as the death of his wife, Priscilla, and the deaths of Leonard Peck and Mary Peck. *I hope that Lady Luck will grace me again.*

He remembered the deaths of the Pecks as if it occurred recently, instead of nineteen years ago. It was on a Friday night and the eve of Glenn's eighteenth birthday. The Pecks drank throughout the week, but indulged on Fridays. They used Saturdays to get sober for Sunday services.

The church and the rectory were located on a dead-end street surrounded by woods. Glenn fantasized as a boy he would run away and live in these woods until his aunt rescued him.

The Pecks were both great actors in the way they transformed on Sundays. Mary would not drink or smoke on either Saturdays or Sundays; however, she smoked non-stop during the week.

Lady Peck sat on the front row of the church on Sundays with the outfits she hung outside on the clotheslines Saturdays to air. As sweet as she looked on Sundays, Glenn could still see the evilness in her face. No one in the church could have ever predicted that under her angelic appearance was the worst demon imaginable.

Glenn recalled the panic he felt when he awoke on the Friday night they died. The smell of smoke burned his eyes and his throat became dry. He tied his pajama top around his nose and ran into the Peck's room. Through the smoke coming from their bed, he could see their bodies. He figured they were drunk as usual, and Mary had dropped a cigarette in the bed. Glenn started to shake them but instead backed out of the room and closed the door.

He returned to his bedroom, retrieved his wooden box, put his robe on, and left the house. Glenn headed to the church, entered through the unlocked back door, and positioned himself in the front pew where he could see his home through the side window. He sat there and thought of the abuse he had suffered from Mary in the eleven years he lived with them and laughed. "God, I guess it's true you move in mysterious ways."

Glenn felt great joy as he sat there and watched the flames dance from the top of the house. After a while, he left his seat and went into the office to call the fire department. *What a great birthday present,* he felt upon receiving confirmation they were both dead.

Peck left him a small insurance policy. It was not much, but it allowed Glenn to make a new start. After their funerals, he packed up Pastor Peck's 1977 Chevy and headed north, hoping he would never have to see Pennsylvania again.

CHAPTER 15

Glenn was in his extravagant house alone as his housekeeper was off for the day. Still recovering from the shock of seeing his aunt, he went to the kitchen and fixed himself a cup of coffee.

Sipping on his coffee, he sat at the table and replayed the last day he had with Priscilla, his late wife. They had been in Baltimore eight months earlier at an award dinner honoring her late father, William Andrew Bolt, the majority stockholder and CEO of a small national bank called the Thrifty Bank. Bolt had died from an accident two years earlier, and his position passed to his only child, Priscilla.

Dinner that Friday night had been in the ballroom of the Arch Hotel, and they were to stay in Bolt's condominium for the weekend. A gift given to Priscilla's father for his help in financing the renovations made to the hotel a few years earlier. Arch hotel had once been a premier place to stay. In the early nineteen hundreds, Woodrow Wilson stayed at the Arch. Numerous celebrities of that time period visited the establishment. The Gale Bar, ballrooms, and the Top Floor nightclub were still open to the public.

Glenn sat at the affair listening to speakers expound the many positive qualities of Priscilla's father. He wished he had met that man instead of the pompous asshole he knew. Glenn almost laughed aloud during the ceremony. Priscilla sat there glowing as if every word uttered was the absolute truth.

To occupy himself, Glenn looked around the ballroom at the renovations. He noticed how the dark wood and the chandeliers remained during the process. The twelfth-floor ballroom had a great view of the city that was spectacular. He hoped that once the affair was over, he could talk Priscilla into going to the Top Floor to listen to jazz.

The ceremony and dinner had ended to Glenn's pleasure and a band began playing. He asked Priscilla to dance, but a few seconds into their dance, she became fatigued.

"Honey, I can't breathe. I need to sit."

"Certainly dear, let's return to the room," Glenn said as he took Priscilla's hand and led her to the elevator. *That's what happens when you marry a woman twenty years older with a heart condition.*

They entered the room. Priscilla looked distressed, and sweat moistened her face. She held her chest, reached into her handbag, and removed a nitroglycerin pill. Glenn hit her hand with such force the pill flew in the air and landed on the other side of the room. He could still see the shocked look on her face as she fell to the floor.

Glenn stood over Priscilla as she took her last breath. He had to work fast as several people had seen them leave together. He removed his clothes and jumped into the shower. After he was wet, he put on a robe and turned Priscilla over on her back. He tore her dress to make it appear he had tried to perform CPR. Satisfied with his efforts, he called the police and the front desk.

Several hours after the ambulance workers left with Priscilla's lifeless body on a stretcher, two black men arrived identifying themselves as detectives.

"May we come in," said the older and heavier of the two men. "My name is Detective Jerome Foster, and my partner is Detective Ray Hollis. I extend my sympathy for your loss, but we need to ask you a few questions."

"Yes, please come in," Glenn said to the two detectives. "May I dress? I was taking a shower when...."

"Take your time," said Detective Foster.

Glenn went into the next room to put on his clothes, but left the door ajar hoping to overhear everything the detectives said.

"I don't know about this, Jerome. How did the nitroglycerin pill get so far from the marker showing the location of her body?" Hollis asked. "It's not as if she dropped it and it bounced or rolled that far on this thick carpet." He got on one knee and patted the floor.

"Please Ray, don't make this difficult. Maybe the police or paramedics kicked it when they came into the room."

"Jerome, those guys are professional. This is not their first night on the job."

"Look Ray, she had a heart condition. She wore a bracelet and her doctor confirmed her condition---what more do you need? These are wealthy people, you may not want your job, but I want mine. I retire in a few weeks and I don't need you making something out of nothing."

Damn I should have picked up that pill from the floor, Glenn thought as he re-entered the room. "Thank you."

"No problem, please tell us what happened," said Detective Foster.

"My wife and I attended an award ceremony for her late father, and she became fatigued, so we returned to our room. I left her, went into the bathroom to take a shower, and told her to rest."

"Where was she when you went into the bathroom?" asked Detective Hollis.

"She was sitting in this chair," Glenn said as he walked over to show where he had moved the chair.

"Did she look as if she was in any distress?" Detective Hollis asked.

"No, she told me she was tired, and I told her to rest. When I came out of the shower, she was on the floor. I turned her over and performed CPR, but I guess it was too late," Glenn said as his voice broke and a tear ran down his face.

"Did you see a nitroglycerin pill in her hand?"

"No, not that I noticed."

"Thank you Mr. Peck. Here's my card if you have any questions," said Detective Foster.

"Thank you," Glenn said as he closed the door behind the detectives.

CHAPTER 16

Glenn continued to sip his coffee and recall the events of the night Priscilla died in Baltimore. After the two detectives left, he went for a walk on the crisp forty-degree December night to calm his nerves and clear his head. He knew he would have to be careful as the sole heir to his wife's estate.

Exiting the hotel, Glenn made a left turn, and walked not paying attention to his surroundings until he came to a bridge and saw a sign that read North 83. Glenn began to turn around but before he could, a scary-looking man came out of the shadows and pointed a knife at his throat.

"Give me your wallet," the man ordered.

Glenn was so afraid he froze.

"Don't think I won't cut you. Give me your wallet," the man repeated.

There was a screech of wheels from a nearby car, and a large, dark figure climbed out of the driver's side and approached the armed man holding a knife pointed to Glenn's neck.

"Didn't anyone ever tell you not to bring a knife to a gun fight," the figure said as he placed a silver object to the back of the knife-yielding-man's head. "Get out of here before I shoot your sorry ass."

The attacker dropped his knife, turned, and ran in the opposite direction.

"Get in the car, Whitey."

Glenn did as instructed. They had driven to the end of the block before Glenn worked up the courage to look at his defender and noticed how much gaudy jewelry he had on his neck and wrists.

"Could you please lower the volume on the radio?" Glenn asked. "Why did you call me Whitey?"

"Don't believe you," the driver chuckled. "I save your life and the only thing you can say is my music is too loud. How about thanks?" He continued, "I asked myself, what white guy is crazy enough to walk up North Avenue wearing a cashmere coat and Gucci Italian leather shoes?" Glenn's rescuer stopped at the red light, turned, and looked at him before continuing. "Your hair is different---lighter, and straighter, figured it may look that way under the streetlights. But I know that walk, on your toes with your head down." He shook his finger at Glenn. "Thirty-some years later and I still have to save your ass," he laughed.

Glenn turned with wide eyes. "Blue, could this be you?"

"It's me, Whitey."

"I'm not called Whitey anymore. My name is Glenn Peck."

"Not called Blue either, but we need to talk," Tommie said as he pulled over in front of the White Corner. "They have the best mini-burgers in here."

Tommie parked the car and walked towards the restaurant. Glenn followed behind thinking this area did not look much better than where the man pulled a knife on him. They entered; Tommie waved at the cook and the waitress behind the counter, and proceeded to the rear. There were four columns of booths on each side of the restaurant, and a narrow aisle separating them. They sat in the last booth with Tommie's back to the wall.

"Where've you been all these years? Why're you going by the name Glenn Peck?" Tommie asked. "Your disappearance really upset your aunt. She searched high and low for you. I heard my momma say she hired a detective to find you."

"She must not have looked too hard. I was in a back-woods place in Pennsylvania for eleven years."

"Man, are you serious? Your aunt tried to find you. It was 1967. Nobody back then was paying attention to what anybody black had to say. She tried."

"I was seven when they took me."

"Yeah, but you didn't stay seven. Where've you been? And why you using the name Glenn Peck?" Tommie asked again. "You know that bastard was your father, and he probably killed your momma. She didn't fall down no steps."

Glenn knew the pastor killed his mother. One night he went into the kitchen, thinking the Pecks were in their bedroom drunk, and found Leonard Peck sitting at the kitchen table with a bottle.

"You have her eyes," he slurred. "I never meant to hurt her. I was trying to keep her from leaving," the drunken man said before he put his head on the table and passed out.

The waitress interrupted Glenn's thoughts as she brought Tommie an order of several little hamburgers and a cup of coffee.

Want a hamburger," Tommie said as he bit into one. "They're the best."

"No, thank you. I'm not hungry," Glenn, answered realizing his childhood friend had not placed an order.

"I'll eat and you talk."

Glenn took a deep breath. "Tommie, we're talking about things that happened a long time ago. Pastor Peck changed my name and told me he'd kill Aunt Pearl and me if I didn't do what he said. I was scared of him and his crazy wife. I stayed because I had no place else to go."

"Your Aunt never left Balmore. I started to search for her when I came here ten years ago, but I didn't think she'd remember me."

"Why'd you leave South Carolina and come to Baltimore?"

"I left my mom and little sister to come up here to get a job at the Bethlehem Steel plant," Tommie answered while still eating his mini burgers. "The pay was good, and I was sending decent money home, but I got laid-off and had a hard time finding another job. My family still needed me so I went into business for myself."

"And what profession is that?"

"Let's say I give people what they want. I guess you could call me a supplier."

"Last I checked that was against the law," Glenn said as he tilted his head and smiled at Tommie.

"Don't talk to me about the law," Tommie responded in a low voice. "What do you know about challenges? You can enter any business and get treated as royalty; you don't know how it is to be looked at with suspicion everywhere you go." Tommie stared at Glenn, before stating, "I don't own no boats, planes, poppy, or marijuana fields. I'm just picking up crumbs left after the politicians get theirs!"

Glenn saw the anger on Tommie's face and looked across the aisle at a man and woman who came into the restaurant and sat in the booth across from them. Tommie stopped eating, looked up from his sandwich, and gave them a hard look. The couple moved to another booth closer to the entrance of the restaurant.

"So how did you get away from the Pecks?"

"They were big drinkers," Glenn answered noting Tommie had changed the conversation. "The church members didn't suspect they were alcoholics. On Sunday, they were sober and holy, but through the week, they drank like fish, especially on Fridays. Glenn shook his head and chuckled. "Mary smoked non-stop and one night she fell asleep with a cigarette in her hand. The bed caught on fire and killed both of them."

"Where were you?"

"I was in my bedroom asleep. By the time I woke up, it was too late. I barely escaped with my life."

"Guess you were lucky."

Glenn did not think he was lucky, and was afraid the whole time he lived with the Pecks. When he was ten, he picked up the telephone in the kitchen and called information. The operator came on the phone, and he asked for the number to his aunt in Baltimore. Before the operator could answer, Mary entered the kitchen, grabbed the phone out of his hand, and beat him. He suffered numerous bruises on his body, a busted lip, and two black eyes. Glenn looked at Tommie and smiled. "I'm not seven anymore and neither are you. We're different people. I appreciate your help tonight. You may have saved my life."

"Look Whitey, Glenn, or whatever you call yourself, I'm not looking for anything from you. I can see you got your thing going on and I got mine. Why were you walking on North Avenue at night dressed as if you're going to a ball?"

"I left a social affair with my wife honoring her late father."

"Your wife? Where is she?"

"She had a heart attack tonight and died. I was walking to clear my head. I wasn't planning on walking, so I didn't have a casual coat or shoes."

"Sorry to hear that. Who's her father?"

"William Bolt."

"William Bolt of the Thrifty Bank?"

Glenn did not expect Tommie to know who William Bolt was. He presumed his childhood friend was not part of the corporate world, and would not know the players. He forgot how smart Tommie was when they were young,

"Look man I'm sorry for your loss," Tommie said. "It's obvious you have things going on, and I'm glad you're alive and well. I take it your wife and her father didn't know your history or heritage?"

"They assumed I'm white, and I told them I was from Philly and my family owned a dry cleaning business."

"So you lied to them. Are you shame of who you are and where you came from?" Tommie asked with a frown on his face.

Glenn could feel the anger mounting inside him. Tommie had some nerve judging him. *As a kid he was so smart, and the best he could do was become a drug dealer.*

"Don't worry," Tommie, said shaking his head. "I got my own thing and don't need unnecessary attention."

"My life is complicated, and like you, I don't need unnecessary attention." Glenn explained as he looked around the restaurant and notice two additional people had entered. "It's better my aunt doesn't know I'm alive. That man not only killed my momma, but the little boy I was. That boy died a long time ago."

"I'll give you my cell number. You and my sister are the only ones that have this number." Tommie wrote his phone number on a card and extended it to Glenn. "If you ever need me, call me. Where're you staying?"

"The Arch Hotel."

"I'll drive you back. Remember man, we may operate in different worlds, but we ain't that different."

"I know Tommie, we never were," Glenn admitted as he took the card and stored it in his wallet. "Once I bury my wife and straighten out some business, I'll call you and give you my number. I really appreciate what you did for me tonight, and if you ever need me...."

"It's okay, you don't owe me anything. I'm glad you're alive. Come on; let me drive you back to the hotel."

CHAPTER 17

Glenn was relieved that Priscilla's death was determined to be from natural causes. He hoped the past was way behind him and now he could concentrate on keeping in touch with his newly found childhood friend until he could figure out what to do about him. Aunt Pearl might become a problem for him; but right now Tommie knew his true name and identity.

He purchased a separate cell phone to keep the lines of communications open between them and made sure no one but Tommie had the phone number. He had spoken to his friend a few times since their reunion several months ago, but he was always the one who initialed the call. It was surprising when Tommie called first, from jail with a major problem.

"I've got myself into a bit of a jam," Tommie said.

Glenn frowned, "What sort of jam?"

"This kid was shooting at me in front of a barbershop. He killed a child and shot an old man. They're charging me with murder and a bunch of other charges."

"What! I heard about that case on the news." Glenn shook his head in disbelief. "Man, that's a mess."

"I need a good lawyer. Can you help me?"

"Do my best. Give me a few days to figure something out." Glenn researched and hired one of the best attorneys in the Baltimore area. He figured this should make them even for the night the man pulled a knife on him, and hoped it was a perfect way to keep Tommie from revealing his identity. Lady Luck had graced him once again.

Three days later, the cell phone he used to talk to Tommie rang. He thought it was odd since he was not expecting a call from jail early in the morning and hesitated before answering.

"Hello."

"Is this Mr. Peck?"

"Yes, who is this?"

"My name is Sheila, Tommie's sister. He told me to call you and let you know the lawyer, Sean Lee Murphy, came to see him yesterday."

"He did?"

"Yes sir and we appreciate it."

"I don't know what he can do. It might just be damage control."

"I know Mr. Peck, but Tommie didn't shoot that man or that little boy in that barbershop. He was protecting himself. It's so unfair," Sheila explained as her voice cracked. "Tommie's in jail and the guy who shot those people, is still on the street."

"It's just a matter of time before the other person is caught, but I'm not sure it matters.

Tommie couldn't have gotten involved in a worst case. Every politician in Baltimore will try to build their career around this case, especially the prosecutor." Glenn heard from Winston that Patty was on the prosecution team. He resumed the conversation with Sheila by adding, "I heard the prosecutor in this case is tough."

"You're right, Mr. Peck. I live two doors from Jay, the prosecutor's assistant, and I heard her tell my next-door neighbor, Thelma, that this was the most important case her boss ever had."

At hearing this, Glenn sat on the edge of his seat and became interested in the conversation. "Does anyone know you're Tommie's sister?"

"No sir. Tommie was very careful not to come to my house or involve me in his business. He didn't want anybody coming after me to get to him."

"How well do you know Jay?"

"Real well, she's a friend of mine.

"Are you sure no one knows you're Tommie's sister?"

"Yes sir, he don't even want me to come to jail or court."

"Good Sheila, keep it that way. I want you to be my eyes and ears. You hear or see anything you call me. If Tommie needs to talk, let him do it through you. I'll buy a cell phone for you, and every so often purchase another phone for both of us, so the numbers won't stay the same. Don't write my number down, memorize it and don't use it to call anyone else but me. Keep the phone with you in case I need to reach you. Do you understand Sheila?"

"Yes sir."

"I'll keep in touch." Glenn smiled as he ended the call and placed the phone on the charger. He was not sure how important the information was that Sheila gave him but was confident he could use it soon.

CHAPTER 18

Asia sat on the love seat in her room listening to the rain hitting the windowpane. There was a loud blast of thunder, and she thought how much the dark rainy weather matched her mood. She kept reading and re-reading the invitation for a bon voyage dinner party in her honor. She looked at the envelope and questioned why Jay did not call instead of mailing the invitation. Asia viewed the invitation again and stared at the picture on the front; it was a picture of her displaying a broad smile. She wondered where Jay had gotten the picture---wherever it came from it was during happier times.

She heard someone climbing the steps to her bedroom and could tell it was Aunt Pearl. Asia could tell the difference between her aunt and uncle's footsteps. In contrast to her uncle, Aunt Pearl's steps were lighter and slower. When Eric was alive, he always ran up and down the stairs. She would tell him to stop, but Eric continued to run. *Guess he knew he wouldn't have time to walk,* Asia thought as the familiar pain hit her again.

Pearl came into Asia's room smiling and holding the invitation to the bon voyage party. "Asia, what are you wearing to your dinner party? It's so nice of Jay to do this for you, isn't it?"

Asia put the invitation on the nightstand and sat on the love seat. "I don't want to go."

"Why not, you leave after Labor Day? I'd think you'd be thrilled."

"I don't understand why we can't do it here, in our home."

"Jay doesn't live here, Asia. What's wrong with her having the dinner at her house?"

"Her house is small, Aunt Pearl."

"How big does her house have to be? It's just you, Patty, me, and Mike."

"And her next-door neighbor, Thelma. You know Jay's inviting her."

"Thelma is a friend. Why do you have a problem with her?"

"She's loud, and she talks too much."

"You must be kidding? You don't want to go to Jay's house because Thelma's loud?"

Pearl sat on the love seat and took Asia's hand. "What do you have against Thelma? Why are you judging her?"

"I hate the way she yells at Marcus."

"Is Marcus her little boy's name?"

"Yes. She has her little boy, my boy is gone!" Asia replied in a screeching voice. "Yet, Thelma yells at him, and I can't stand it. I won't be around her," she added as she cried.

Pearl walked over to the sculpture of a boy giving his mother flowers and caressed it. "It's hard to lose someone you love, particularly your child, but Thelma had nothing to do with Eric's death. You can't be angry with Thelma because God took Eric home."

"God! Don't talk about God. Where was God when two thugs shot at each other in front of a barbershop and killed my sweet baby? Where was He?" Asia screamed as tears streamed down her face.

Pearl walked over to her niece and grabbed her hand. "Please come to the window."

Reluctantly, Asia stood and followed Pearl to the window.

"Look up at the sky. What do you see?"

"I see clouds. It's raining, Aunt Pearl. I see rain clouds."

"Do you see the sun?"

"No, it's raining. The sun is not shining." Asia answered curtly.

"Does that mean there's no sun since you can't see it, or does it mean you can't see the sun right now because of the clouds?"

"I don't know. I guess it's because the sun is covered by the clouds."

"The sun's still there, Asia. It hasn't fallen out of the sky, and the earth is still revolving around it." Pearl held on to her niece's hand and looked into her face. "We had a saying when I was a young woman; you have to keep on, keeping on."

"What does that mean?" Asia asked, not in the mood for one of her aunt's sayings that made no sense to her.

"It means you have to wake up every day expecting to breathe and feel the warmth and love from people who love you. It means you have to keep doing whatever it takes to get through the minefield called *life*. This is without a doubt the hardest thing you'll ever experience. I don't know why Eric died." Pearl let out a sigh. "I know it's not fair, and it's not your fault. I also know Eric was a loving, happy little boy. As difficult as it may sound, you are not the first person to lose their child, and you won't be the last."

Pearl took Asia's face in her hands, as she continued, "I'm not trying to be hard on you honey, but you'll need faith to get through this. Don't tarnish Eric's memory with bitterness in your heart and please don't nurse your hurt. I wish I could tell you something that makes sense of this, but I can't---there's no magic formula to fix this. You won't get over this in a month or a year. The pain you're experiencing *cuts like a knife*. Maybe, one day the joy of having Eric will overcome the pain of losing him."

She cupped her niece's chin and forced Asia to look her in the eye. "If you are taking this job in Boston to run away from your pain, forget it. You can't outrun your pain. Everywhere you go, you take yourself with you. Let Jay do this for you. She wants to show you she loves you. Don't judge Thelma. You don't know her story," Pearl said as she wrapped her arms around Asia's shoulders.

Sobbing, Asia fell into her aunt's arms. The only sound in the room was the heavy rain beating on the windowpane. Her aunt had never talked to her this way. "I'll try Aunt Pearl," she murmured between tears, "I'll try."

CHAPTER 19

The month of August was holding on to its summer heat until the last day. It was early evening, and the thermostat had dropped five points to a cool ninety degrees. *At least the shade is on this side of the street;* Sheila thought as she sat bare-footed and curled up on her lounge chair, watching her neighbors' children playing in the park across the street from her house. Kiki was barking orders at Marcus to push her higher on the swing, and the boy was attentive to her every need.

Sheila heard music blasting as soon as Thelma opened her front door, singing loud, and as usual off-key. *What she lacks in talent, she makes up for in volume.*

Thelma stopped singing and looked across the street at the park. "Marcus! Bring Kiki over here and come in the house. She looked at Sheila, "Boy ain't got sense enough to come in out the sun."

Sheila pointed her finger at Thelma and laughed. "They kids, and don't get hot as your old butt does."

"Old?" Thelma frowned. "Ain't nothing old about this fine butt," she said smacking her side.

"You're a trip. Where's Jay?"

"At the market buying food with money she don't have to host a dinner party for Queen Asia."

"Be nice, Thelma. Asia lost her little boy, remember?" Sheila wondered how Thelma and Jay would treat her if they knew her brother was involved in the shooting that took Eric's life.

"You're right. I don't mean to say anything bad about Asia, especially after what happened to her little boy. I'd go crazy if that had been Marcus, but Asia acts as if she's royalty, and she cleans offices for a living."

"Too bad everybody can't keep it real like you Thelma," Sheila replied.

"Oh, you got jokes," Thelma said pointing her finger at Sheila. "Jay tries so hard to please people. She's driving herself crazy over this party. On top of the food, she wants me to help her paint the front door and bannister. Jay's talking about getting up at six o'clock tomorrow morning." She placed her hands on her hips. "I don't do six o'clock on Saturday morning unless I'm coming in from Friday night."

"Shut up," Sheila laughed. "Who's coming to this dinner party?"

Thelma held up an imaginary checklist as she recited, "Asia, her aunt and uncle, and of course the mighty Ms. Patty. I'm coming to help Jay with the cooking."

"I know that's right," Sheila said waving her hand. "Jay has lots of fine qualities, but cooking ain't one of them. What type of people are Asia's aunt and uncle? I've gone to Asia's house with Jay to pick up Kiki, but I've never had much conversation with them."

"They're the sweetest people you ever want to meet. Ms. Pearl is real nice and Mr. Mike is cool for an old guy."

Sheila laughed, "You better watch your-self, you know what they say. Just because there's snow on the roof doesn't mean there isn't fire in the furnace."

Thelma bent over laughing, "Where do you get these old-folk sayings?"

Sheila's mother used old clichés and idioms as if it was second nature. Her mother would say that some people were similar to bananas; you had to peel back the layers to see them. That was Thelma; it took a while to get to know her. She appeared hard sometimes but would be the first to help someone. Sheila's mother, like Thelma, was loud and did not bite her tongue.

The new cell phone Mr. Peck sent Sheila rang from inside the house. She forgot and left the phone on the coffee table in the living room. She jumped up out of the lounge chair and rushed to the front door. "I'll be right back."

"Who's got you running to the phone?" Thelma asked.

Sheila ignored Thelma as she rushed into her house to answer her cell phone. "Hello," she answered out of breath.

"What took you so long to answer the phone?" Glenn asked.

"I was on the porch talking to my neighbor. We were talking about Jay having a dinner party for her friend, and I forgot to take the phone with me." She apologized, not wanting to upset him.

"That's fine Sheila. You say Jay is having a dinner party. She's the prosecutor's secretary?"

"Yes sir, it's for Asia, the mother of the little boy that died. She's going to Boston for a new job."

"That's nice of Jay. Who's coming to this dinner party?"

"It will be Asia, her aunt and uncle, Jay's boss, and Thelma, my next-door neighbor."

"Are you going to the party?"

"No sir. Did you want something?" Sheila asked wondering why he was asking questions about Jay's party.

"I wanted to check to see if you had spoken to Tommie."

"Yes sir. He has a motion hearing next week."

"Have they caught the other guy, the one who tried to shoot Tommie?"

"No, sir."

"Does Tommie know his name?"

"Tommie just knows his street name is Mad Dog."

"When you talk to Tommie again, tell him I'm doing everything I can. What time is the dinner party?"

Sheila hesitated as she thought his question was strange. Again, she wondered why he was asking about Jay's dinner party.

"It should start around seven."

"Thank you and stay strong."

"Yes sir, goodbye."

The young woman had an uncertain feeling regarding the conversation she had with her brother's friend, and remembered Tommie told her to be careful what she told Mr. Peck because people had a mysterious way of dying around him. She shook it off as she went back on the porch to talk to Thelma.

Glenn could not believe his good luck. Patty, Asia, Uncle Mike, and Aunt Pearl under one roof at the same time, all the players who could hurt him, he thought and smiled. He devised a simple plan to take care of Aunt Pearl knowing his identity and possibly sharing it with anyone else. To accomplish his goal, he needed to find Mad Dog and hire a private investigator.

During his research, he came across a name and phone number of an investigator who had worked for the police department in Baltimore for over twenty-five years. Glenn figured the ex-officer still had connections and could track Mad Dog, or someone connected to him with no problem. The name of the investigator was Jerome Foster, which sounded familiar. Glenn looked through his papers and saw Jerome Foster's name on the card one of the detectives gave him the night Priscilla died.

Glenn did a credit check on Foster and found out the investigator had two loans with the Thrifty Bank. There was a risk, and Glenn wondered if he should still use Foster, but decided there was no reason for them to meet in person. Glenn would use Brian Adams, when conducting business with him over the phone. In addition, Foster's financial situation made him worth the risk. Lady Luck was still with Glenn.

CHAPTER 20

Jerome Foster felt queasy as he sat behind his desk looking at a pile of overdue notices. Nausea was threatening to cause an eruption from his stomach every time he looked at the big bold **overdue** words. The Thrifty Bank hit him the hardest; he had taken out a second equity loan on his home to start his business. If Jerome did not make a mortgage payment, his business, and home could be in jeopardy.

He hid this financial information from his wife, Dana. Jerome loved her with all his heart and did not want to burden her. He had made many mistakes with two previous wives, and could not afford to lose his third wife. Even after ten years together, there were times he could not believe she was his. Dana made him feel as if he were the luckiest man in the world.

Jerome opened Results Investigations seven months ago, a month after he retired from the police department. He worked in the patrol unit in west Baltimore for twenty years and spent the last five in the Homicide Unit. Several people patted Jerome on the back and said they would bring him work once he started his business. He thought he would receive a big contract from a group of small insurance companies, but another firm offered them a better deal.

In the beginning, everything fell into place with his new business venture. He got a loan and found a great office location on a major street in a strip mall with easy access and parking right in front of the building. The Ashburton Eye Care occupied his space, but moved next door to a bigger location. Jerome met the owner when he purchased prescription sunglasses. They clicked, and the owner helped Jerome negotiate a good price for his lease.

He sat at his desk and continued looking at his bills in horror. *Breathe and calm down* he told himself. The only sound in the small two-room office was from Sayda, his stepdaughter, typing on her computer in the reception area. She had to be playing a game he reasoned as he had not given her any work, and when he gave her work, she was not that diligent.

Jerome disliked his stepdaughter and hired her to make his wife happy. She had none of the fine qualities his wife possessed. Dana was a real woman who cared for others, and Sayda cared for herself.

It was two o'clock on a Friday afternoon and the phone had not rung all day. Jerome picked up the phone several times to make sure it was still connected. When the phone rang, Jerome grabbed it before Sayda could answer.

"Results Investigations, may I help you?"

"May I speak to Jerome Foster?"

"Speaking."

"Mr. Foster, my name is Brian Adams, and I understand you locate people."

"Yes, I do. Who are you trying to find?"

"You were a police officer in Baltimore City for many years, weren't you?"

"Twenty-five years." Jerome answered with pride. "What can I do for you?"

"I'm looking for someone who I know either lives in or frequents Baltimore."

"Do you have any details on this person?" Jerome asked as he reached for a pad and a pen.

"I have his street name---Mad Dog."

Jerome frowned, dropped his pen, and sat back in his chair. "Is this the same Mad Dog involved in a shooting about two months ago? If it is, every cop in Baltimore City is looking for him."

"I don't need you to find him, just someone close to him--mother, father, or brother. You get the picture?"

"Why do you need someone close to him?"

"It is important that I deliver a letter to him or to someone that could give it to him. I'm willing to pay handsomely for the delivery."

"What do you consider handsome?"

"Five-thousand dollars, two thousand up front and the rest after the letter is delivered, but it must be delivered today."

"Today," he exclaimed. "It's two o'clock in the afternoon." Jerome looked at his watch to be sure. "How can I deliver a letter today?"

"The letter is being special delivered to you, and should be there shortly."

Jerome sat on the edge of his chair and gripped the receiver to his ear. "Wait a minute,

Mr. Adams," he said in stern voice. "Aren't you being presumptuous? What in the world makes you think I would accept this assignment? I'm not the post office, and I don't know what's in *your* letter that is worth five-thousand dollars to deliver!"

"I can assure you Mr. Foster, there're no drugs or anything illegal involved. Pull up your on-line bank account and you will see that two thousand has been deposited into your account."

Jerome turned to his desktop computer and logged into his bank account. He checked his account and sure enough, his account showed a two-thousand dollar deposit. Perplexed, Jerome spoke into the receiver in a shaky voice. "How did...you get the money...in my account? I didn't give you my account number."

"Please hold on Mr. Foster."

Glenn put the phone on hold. "I have to calm down," he said aloud while rubbing his forehead. "I may have made a mistake putting the money in his account." He took the phone off hold. "Mr. Foster you don't have to accept this job or the money," Glenn said as he returned to the phone.

Jerome thought about not taking this job. He did not have to be a retired police officer to know something was not right with this situation, but he needed this money. Five-thousand dollars would be a help.

"I...know where his mother lives," Jerome hesitated before adding, "I can deliver the letter to her."

"You can't open the letter, and you need her signature."

"When will I receive the letter?"

"It should be there soon."

"How will I reach you to let you know I delivered the letter?"

"I'll call you back in three hours, Mr. Foster."

As soon as Jerome hung up the phone, a carrier walked into the investigator's office with a package.

"I need to deliver this package to Jerome Foster," the carrier told Sayda.

"I'll get it," Jerome yelled from his office, overhearing the carrier's exchange. He got up from his desk, walked over to his stepdaughter's desk, and signed for the package. He waited until the carrier left his office before he looked at the envelope for any clues of its contents.

"What's that?"

"Work," Jerome replied. He reached for his sports jacket on the coat rack in the corner of his office, but decided he did not need a jacket where he was going.

"I'll be back soon," he said before he exited the office. He knew Sayda would leave at five o'clock on the dot whether he was back or not.

***

"Good riddance!" Sayda shouted as soon as Jerome closed the outside door. She was so glad her stepfather left the office; his *woe is me* demeanor was really getting on her nerves. She thought he should have been out drumming up business rather than sitting there waiting for it to come to him. She knew he hired her because of Dana---a woman he did not deserve.

Her mother could have done much better than Jerome Foster for a husband. Dana should have been with a doctor, lawyer, senator---anybody but an ex-cop with an attitude working on his third marriage. Cops viewed everyone as potential suspects, guilty of something. What was the attraction she wondered? At five feet ten, Jerome had a stocky build with a bulging belly. In contrast, Dana was a natural beauty, who did not need fake hair, or acrylic nails; and maintained her petite size-six body frame. More important than her outward appearance, was her kindness.

Sayda hoped her mother had not put any hard-earned money into Jerome's doomed investigation business. She could not open the mail, but knew that most of what came in were bills, not checks. She thought his experience could have gotten him a security job. *Mr. Big Shot had to open his own business* she thought looking at her resume on the computer. Sayda hoped his business did not sink before she found another job.

CHAPTER 21

Jerome drove about fifteen minutes to where he thought Mad Dog's mother, Tisha might be at this time of day. As he drove, he thought of her from when he was a young police officer, and she was a kid in the neighborhood he patrolled. At that time, she was cute and sweet; but several years later, she became hooked on heroin. He remembered how she turned into a person who no longer had any resemblance to the young sweet girl he once knew.

Macy, Tisha's mother, occupied his thoughts as he drove. He also met her while he was in patrol. Jerome had married three times, and he loved his third wife, but Macy was very special. Jerome remember how beautiful she was, inside and out with her curvy soft body and a face stunning enough to make any super model jealous. Jerome felt God made a mistake by making Macy human. She should have been a magnificent bird, sitting high in the mountains under a tree that would protect her from any harm.

Jerome thought how little joy Macy had in her life at that time. She took care of a mean old ailing father, her daughter chased drugs, and Macy was raising Tisha's baby. Yet, she never appeared bitter. Nothing seemed to discourage her until the night Tisha was badly beaten.

Still driving, Jerome reflected on that night. He was on duty and received the call. Tisha went to the hospital with a broken nose, broken ribs, and two black eyes. She refused to say who hurt her, but he knew who the dealers were in her neighborhood. He put the word out if anyone else tried to hurt her or her family, he would make business very difficult for them.

Jerome returned to Macy's house several days later to check on Tisha and see if she was ready to say who hurt her. Macy opened the front door, let him in, and guided him into the living room. Her grandson was on her hip crying, Tisha was in the next room screaming for her, and the father was upstairs yelling Macy's name. It reminded Jerome of a scene out of a B-rated horror movie. He took the baby from Macy, and told her to go check on her daughter and father, and he could wait a few minutes to talk to Tisha.

By the time Macy returned to the living room, Jerome had rocked the baby to sleep. She took the baby from him and tried to express her gratitude before bursting into tears. Jerome knew that was his clue to leave, but she looked so distraught, fragile, and beautiful. He took the baby from her and placed him in the playpen in the corner of the room. Jerome gently put his arms around Macy and felt her trembling. They made love on the living room floor resembling two drowning people trying to reach shore. Their love affair was doomed from the beginning. Jerome was having marital problems with his first wife. They also had to be careful in public, besides being married, it was a violation for an officer to have an intimate relationship with someone who lived in the community they patrolled. It was hard and it hurt, but Jerome somehow found the strength to end their affair. He knew it broke Macy's heart.

Snapping back from his thoughts, Jerome pulled up in front of Pee Wee's Watering Hole. Folks in the neighborhood called the bar, *The Hole in the Wall*. He always told people the place lived up or down to that name depending on your perspective. He parked his car and walked into the bar taking off his designer prescription sunglasses. It was always dark in this bar, even in the daytime. The windows stayed covered to keep the sunlight out, and it smelled as dark as it looked---a battle between old urine, vomit, and Pine-Sol; with the urine and vomit winning. He heard blues playing in the background, and the music matched the decorum. This was the most depressing place he had ever been.

The bar was small, and the front of it was narrow. There was a counter to the right of the entrance with seats for ten to twelve people. One person at a time could walk by the counter and stools if patrons were at the bar. There was a larger room on the other side of the bar with eight small tables and four chairs at each table. Beyond this room, was a closet-sized area with a rod and heavy dark curtains at the entrance. Jerome felt sure this was where he would find Tisha.

Pee Wee was behind the bar where he was every time Jerome came into this place. He wondered if Pee Wee ever went home or to the bathroom.

"You can't go back there!" Pee Wee shouted with his slurred speech and missing teeth. "You ain't no police no more."

"Shut up Pee Wee. I'm looking for Tisha, and I'm sure she's back there."

"I ain't seen her."

"If she's not back there, then you don't mind if I take a look."

"Come on Foster, cut the girl a break."

Jerome snared at Pee Wee and kept moving. Just as he reached for the curtain, a well-dressed man came pushing and rushing past Jerome, almost knocking him to the floor.

Taking a deep breath, Jerome barged in as Tisha was getting up from a kneeled position.

She frowned, before screaming, "What the fu..."

"Before you start with your gutter mouth, I have an envelope for you. Somebody paid me good money to give it to you." Jerome knew if Tisha thought she was getting something of value, she would calm down.

"It better be, Foster. I don't have time for your shit. I'm not my mother."

"What I tell you about your gutter mouth? And what happened between me and your mother is none of your business," Jerome said as he pointed his finger at Tisha. "Go into the bathroom, clean yourself up, and come talk."

Tisha rolled her eyes at Jerome before she went to the restroom. When she came out, she sat on the opposite side of him with a scowl on her face. Jerome handed her a paper to sign. He removed the letter sized-envelope from inside the larger envelope that had his address on it before he left his car. He did not want to give Tisha any reason to become suspicious of this transaction. "Here Tisha, sign this and you can have this envelope." Jerome took a pad out of his folder, and wrote that he delivered the sealed package to Tisha Evans, and he drew a line for her to date and sign her name. He wished he had Sayda type a formal receipt notice before he left the office, so it could look more professional.

She looked at the envelope, frowned, and turned to Jerome. "What's in this?"

"I don't know. I left my x-ray glasses at home."

Tisha rolled her eyes. "You're too damn smart."

"Just sign the paper, so I can get out of this rat hole."

"Why should I? It could be something bad. Maybe somebody is suing me."

"Please, you ain't got nothing. Besides, it must be important because you're supposed to give it to Lamont."

"Oh, now I'm stupid," she said swerving her head. "You must think it runs in the family. If I took this letter to Lamont, you or some other pig would follow me."

"Watch your mouth." Jerome admonished. "I'm not a police officer anymore. I don't care what you think of me, or do with this envelope." He pushed the form in front of Tisha to sign. "You can stick it for all I care. I want you to sign and take it. Give it to Lamont or throw it in the trash."

"I don't want my son to get into more trouble."

"You picked a good time to be concerned about your son. If it weren't for him trying to keep your junkie ass out of that back room, he would've never sold drugs."

Jerome saw the hurt flash across Tisha's face. *Maybe there is an ounce of decency left in her.* She was still young, but her appearance made her look years older. Tisha appeared sickly with a small and thin physique, her light-brown complexion was dull and ashy. She had big bags under her eyes, and two of her front teeth were missing.

"Fuck you!" Tisha snatched the paper from Jerome, dated it, and scribbled her signature on the dotted line.

"Thank you very much," Jerome said rolling his eyes, as he handed the envelope to Tisha and left the bar.

***

Tisha sat and held the envelope in her hand--- just staring at it. She turned it several times, trying to decide if she should open it. After a few minutes, she got up and went to the ladies' room carrying it with her. Once inside she opened the letter-sized envelope, ripped it open, and took out a single sheet with one line typed on it. She moved close to the light and read the one line. Tisha sat on the side of the sink in the two-stall bathroom and read the letter again but aloud. "The main witness and the lead prosecutor will be at 1289 Delair Road tomorrow, Saturday evening between the hours of seven o'clock and approximately nine o'clock."

She did not know what to do with this information. Tisha read it several times before she understood what it meant. She knew in her heart that her son did not mean to kill that little boy, or shoot that old man. Tisha wondered if she should give this information to her son, or could it make his situation worse? *Oh hell, it can't get any worse,* she thought as she went to the pay phone in the bar, called her son, and read the contents of the letter.

CHAPTER 22

Asia stood in front of her bedroom dresser putting on makeup for her going-away party. She looked in the mirror and saw how pretty she appeared in her orange and yellow skirt set that complimented her deep brown complexion.

"Are you ready yet?" Pearl called from the second floor. "We don't want to be late for your party."

"Almost," Asia replied and exhaled deeply. "I should be ready in five minutes."

"We'll wait for you in the living room."

Asia's aunt and uncle were waiting for her as she entered the room. Having her aunt and uncle in her life during this trying time made it possible to withstand the awful pain of losing her child. She felt tears coming to her eyes, but knew she had to hold them back because she did not want her aunt and uncle to think they were tears of sorrow.

She eyed the cake holder in her aunt's hands and hoped it was a red velvet cake. No one made red velvet cake as good as Aunt Pearl did. She glanced at the bouquet of yellow roses in her uncle's hand; he found out from Patty that they were Jay's favorite.

Mike stepped toward his niece and gave her a hug. "Don't worry; we'll have a good time."

"I know," Asia said as she noticed her uncle's hair was grayer than she remembered; and there was a slight droop to his shoulders on his six-foot frame. She had not thought about how much Eric's death affected her aunt and uncle. Uncle Mike was the only father Eric knew. Harry's paternal act was calling her names after their son died. One day they might need her to help them as they had always been there for her. Would she be able to do so, she wondered?

As hard as it was, Asia had to admit she had not accomplished much on her own. Her uncle got her the cleaning job at the courthouse because he knew the owners of the cleaning business, Colonel James and his daughter, Eileen. Uncle Mike often bragged how Colonel James was a retired colonel from the army and was giving back to the community. Asia believed Patty was responsible for Augustus offering her the job taking care of his children. Aunt Pearl kept Eric while she worked and Eric spent a great deal of time with his great aunt and uncle.

Mike stood back and smiled at Asia and Pearl. "I may have to take a big stick with me to beat back the guys so I can take you two beautiful women out the front door."

Pearl giggled as a schoolgirl and Asia smiled in spite of herself.

"Come, my ladies," Mike said as he extended his arms to Pearl and Asia. He escorted them to his ten-year-old car, which he kept looking as if it had just come off the show-room floor.

During the short ride to Jay's house, Asia listened to them singing to the oldies playing on the radio. Anxiety built in her stomach as her mind drifted back to the photographs of the elegantly dressed performers on the walls of Joe's barbershop. *How could a special day for Eric end so tragically?*

Asia felt so much resentment over losing her precious child. She was angry with the two men who sold drugs, and the people who used drugs, making it profitable. She blamed the politicians who closed their eyes and benefited from the criminal activity in the black community. Most of her anger and resentment was with God for not protecting Eric from a senseless death. She wanted to scream, but instead sat back in the seat and closed her eyes, so her aunt and uncle could not see her pain. When she opened her eyes, her uncle was parking in front of Jay's house.

She regretted she did not want to come after she saw the work Jay had done to make the party special. The banister and the door were painted, and the grass freshly cut. Asia wondered if Jay cut it with her push mower.

The front door of Jay's house led into the living room, and the house was spotless. Asia could see the dining room and the kitchen. The dining room table had an attractive setting that Jay matched from various second-hand and thrift stores.

"Hi," Jay said as she walked out of the kitchen, and gave Asia, Mike and Pearl hugs. "I'm glad you all made it."

"We wouldn't miss it for the world," Pearl replied with a broad smile. "Where can I put this cake?"

"I'll put it in the kitchen with the rest of the food. Dinner will be ready soon."

Asia saw Thelma in the kitchen cooking. Asia had to admit the aroma was making her hungry. Thelma had her faults, but she was a great cook.

"These are for you," Mike said, handing Jay the bouquet of roses.

Jay blushed and smiled, "Wow... they're so pretty. Thank you so much, I'll put them in a vase. Everyone have a seat in the living room, and I'll let you know when the food is ready."

Asia noticed how pleased her friend appeared when Uncle Mike gave her the flowers. Jay was a mystery; she never talked to Asia about having a boyfriend, or anything other than her child. She told how Kiki's father died before his child was born, but the child was five years old. That was a long time to be alone, especially for someone as beautiful as Jay.

Patty was talking to Marcus regarding school while Kiki stood on the side watching them. It amazed Asia how a child could be as bright as Marcus and have Thelma for his mother.

Jay entered the living room again, "Dinner will be ready soon, is anyone interested in cocktails?"

"Yes, as soon as the kids go upstairs," Patty answered.

"Sure, it's time for them to go. They've had their dinner." Jay turned to her daughter, "Kiki you and Marcus go upstairs and watch the movie I bought today."

After the kids left the room, Jay wheeled out an attractive little cart that contained a bottle of Hennessey for Mike, Absolut vodka for Patty, and a bottle of wine for Pearl and Asia. It also had a bottle of coke, small cranberry juice, glasses, and a small ice bucket. Jay had what each of them preferred to drink.

The atmosphere was pleasant. Mike was telling jokes, and they were laughing, listening to music, and having a good time. Asia replayed the conversation she had with Aunt Pearl about running away from herself. She laughed when everyone else did, but her mind was a thousand miles away. More than once, she questioned whether she should leave to go to Boston.

"Dinner's ready." Thelma announced from the kitchen.

Everyone stood and walked toward the dining table while Jay and Thelma arranged several casserole dishes and a platter of roasted chicken and beef in the center of it.

"Everything looks great," Asia said in amazement.

"I hope you enjoy it. We want to send you off with a full belly," Jay said as everyone laughed.

Asia sat back in her chair after finishing her meal. "Jay, this dinner was so delicious, I haven't eaten this much food in a long time. I feel as if I could burst," Asia laughed while rubbing her stomach. Again, she felt ashamed of herself for not wanting to come.

"I'm glad you enjoyed it," Jay said with a grin. "Are you guys ready for Ms. Pearl's red velvet cake and coffee?"

"Bring it on," laughed Mike. "I'm not sure where I'll put it, but will do my best."

"Please count me in," Patty answered. "I'm hitting the gym tomorrow morning.

"What about you Ms. Pearl and Asia?"

"I'll take a small piece," Pearl answered.

Asia explained, "I think I ate too much. Do you mind if I sit on the front porch and grab some air for a few minutes?"

"Of course not, are you all right? Should you take anything?"

"No, everything was so good I ate like a pig. I need a couple of minutes to digest my food, but I'm taking a piece of cake home with me."

Asia left the kitchen table and walked out onto the front porch. Closing the door behind her, she could still hear the laughter coming from inside the house. She needed to spend a few minutes alone, not just because she over ate, which was a good excuse, but because she felt overwhelmed. Asia was not sure she should go to Boston, but staying in the same area her son died was painful and unbearable.

Pacing the small porch trying to make a decision, Asia glanced across the street and listened to the crickets chirping in the park. The porch light was off, and she relied on the streetlight in front of the park to illuminate the darkness. She spotted several people, walking pass Jay's house but doubted they could see her.

Asia stopped pacing and took advantage of the quiet night. She sat in a chair on the porch and closed her eyes. Her eyes opened when someone drove their car in front of Jay's house and stopped for a few seconds before pulling away. She sat up on the edge of the chair trying to identify the driver without success. Her curiosity intensified when the same car returned and parked across the street in front of the park.

CHAPTER 23

Lamont Tyne street name Mad Dog, a title he preferred sat in his car in front of the park planning his next move, and reviewed the address his mother read over the phone to make sure he was at the right place. There was a dim light radiating from the window of the house, and he could see shadows of people. Mag Dog had her read the letter three times before he understood what it meant.

Nothing regarding this situation was the way he had planned and he wondered why someone would go to so much trouble to give him the whereabouts of the prosecutor out to put him behind bars and the main witness who could place him at the scene of the crime. He worried he was being set-up since the police could not find him.

The young man had been in Baltimore City the whole time, hiding out in his aunt's attic. His aunt had a big old house in the Junction, a neighborhood fifteen to twenty minutes away from the barbershop where the shooting took place. Twice the police came to his aunt's house looking for him, but did not find him hiding right in the attic. He had to do something; he could not hide in his aunt's attic forever. She was letting him stay because he was paying her, but as soon as the money was gone, he knew she would kick him out, or if one of his cousins got into trouble, they would tell on him to save themselves.

Tisha's son heard his mother had returned to Pee Wee's back room. At one time, he thought about killing Pee Wee, but figured it might not have done any good. At least she was safe at Pee Wee's bar. No one would harm her there and chance dealing with Mad Dog. Even as a boy, he knew what his mother did in that back room. As he became older, he tried to get her off drugs, and enrolled her into several programs. She might stay a few days or hours and then leave.

After a while he conceded, she was hooked on heroin, which was why he never sold it. He preferred to sell marijuana and crack cocaine, and told himself crack did not create physical addiction and weed never hurt anyone. He ignored the awful reality that people became as addicted to crack as his mother was to heroin.

He meant to scare Tommie the day he shot at him entering the barbershop and did not mean to hurt Mr. Joe or kill that little boy. His east side rival had disrespected him by selling drugs on his turf, and it was not the first time. There was an understanding that Tommie sold drugs on the east side, and he sold drugs on the west side. Colby was once one of Mad Dog's best customers before he started working at the barbershop with Mr. Joe. The former supplier did not believe Colby had stopped smoking weed. Tommie must have driven past twenty barbershops to come to west Baltimore to get his hair cut. They must have thought he was crazy not to know Colby was getting his drugs from Tommie. *I had to act, he forced my hand,* Mad Dog thought as he sat in his car.

If he had let anyone get away with that level of disrespect, his homeboys be calling him little "puppy" instead of Mad Dog. He had enough problems because of his small physique and light complexion; he could not let *that man* punk him on that level and maintain any respect.

Mad Dog sat thinking how everything he had worked for disappeared after the shooting. He hoped the fewer number of people who could identify him, the better. He figured the mother of the little boy had to be the one that fingered him. He did not think it was anyone else in the barbershop. Tommie would look weak by snitching. The other people would not want to get involved, so that left the little boy's mother.

He had given this situation considerable thought and decided he would throw a firebomb at the front porch as a scare tactic. The people in the house should have plenty of time to get out through the back door before the house caught on fire, he concluded. "Yeah," he said nodding his head. "After this happens, they'll know I'm not someone they want to cross."

Taking a deep breath, Mag Dog turned off the ignition, and climbed out his car. He opened the trunk, grabbed the gas can, and an empty soda bottle. He sat them on the curb and poured enough gasoline into the bottle to fill it halfway.

He returned to his trunk, removed a rag, and immersed it into the bottle of gasoline.

Satisfied with his version of a firebomb, he put the gasoline can back into his trunk, closed it, and removed a cigarette lighter out of his back pocket. Mag Dog was nervous as he crossed the street and walked toward the house with the bottle of gasoline in one hand and the lighter in the other.

He lit the rag and saw a slight movement from a shadow on the porch as he approached. Something hard hit him in the head with such force it knocked him to the ground. The bottle he held in his hand broke and covered him with gasoline. He was on fire! The young man rolled around trying to put it out. The pain was so excruciating. He was afraid and felt he was going to die. He welcomed death if it could stop this agonizing pain.

Tisha's child was not afraid of dying, but of leaving his mother. How could she take care of herself without him? He had taken care of her most of his life. He was the parent, and she was the child. Mag Dog knew the world saw her as a low-life junkie, but he loved her.

His grandmother had taught him about God, and she took him to church when he was a boy; but he did not give much thought to such things. God did nothing for him or his mother; but still he prayed. "Forgive me and please take care of my mother."

After Lamont (Mag Dog) Tyne prayed, he felt peaceful and closed his eyes.

CHAPTER 24

Detective Ray Hollis was surprised to receive a call from Patty since they were not working on a case together. She sounded frazzled, which was unusual for her. On the worse cases they worked together, Patty was always cool and controlled. Ray heard her say *firebomb at Jay's house*, and he was out the door. He hoped he had not hung up on her.

He knew the situation was dire based on the panicky sound of Patty's voice. He drove his car fast, as if he was a speed racer. His heart was pounding as he worried about *his* Jay; he cared for her but was too afraid to let her know.

Judges, attorneys, and police approached the prosecutor and her assistant. Patty swatted them like flies, but Jay would smile and decline their advances. Ray believed if she rejected some of them, he did not stand a chance, and his heart could not take the pain. He was a divorcee with a difficult ex-wife and a young son who had seen too many bad exchanges between his parents.

Ray wondered what he could offer a woman like Jay.

He parked his car as the ambulance sped away, and the uniformed officers were still on the scene. Ray approached Patty, who was wringing her hands and pacing back and forth on the porch. She looked worse than she had sounded on the phone. Her eyes were red, and her makeup smeared.

"What's going on?"

"A guy had a firebomb in his hand to throw at Jay's house, but Asia was sitting on the porch and threw a rock and hit him. He dropped the gasoline-filled bottle and caught on fire," Patty stated in one breath.

"Who's the guy? And why would he throw a firebomb at Jay's house?"

"I'm not sure, but I heard an officer say they thought it was Mad Dog, or what's left of him."

"Patty, how'd he know where Jay lived, and how was it he picked a night when you and Asia were here at the same time?"

"That's the million dollar question," Patty answered. "I'm going to the hospital, but he may not be able to talk yet."

"Is everyone okay?"

"Everyone's fine except Asia's Uncle Mike's hand got burned trying to save the bastard's life."

"Where's Asia's uncle?"

"His wife drove him to the hospital."

"He must be a good man," Ray said shaking his head. "I don't think I'd have lifted a finger to help that murderer."

"Uncle Mike didn't know who he was, not that it would've mattered."

Ray nodded. "You go ahead to the hospital and I'll talk to Asia to see what she has to say."

"Be gentle, Ray. She's been through a lot."

"I will and you're right, she has. I'll meet you at the hospital after I talk to her."

As Detective Hollis entered Jay's house, he saw Thelma with her arms around Asia helping her drink a glass of water. He thought about asking Thelma to leave, but Asia was holding on to her for dear life.

He met Thelma once in Patty's office, and she left quite an impression on him. He remembered that day very well. Jay interrupted him and Patty preparing for a trial, to ask if she could take a longer lunch break and meet with her friend, Thelma.

Her enthusiasm surprised Ray, as she was quiet and reserved even in the way she dressed. Jay wore conservative, loose-fitting clothing, and Ray wondered if it was a failed attempt to hide her hourglass shape and long shapely legs.

Thelma was not reserved or attempted to downplay anything. He heard her before he saw her in Patty's reception room. Thelma had on skintight jeans stretched to the maximum, and she had quite a bit to put into them. Her top barely covered her breast, which he knew did not allow her to see her feet when she was standing straight, and had a gold crown on her front tooth. Ray could not understand why Baltimore women wore gold teeth. He thought Thelma and Jay made an interesting looking pair.

"What in the world was that?" Ray asked Patty after Thelma and Jay left for lunch.

"They are friends, and Jay likes her," Patty replied as she threw up both hands.

Ray took a deep breath and shook off his thoughts of Thelma. He sat in a chair across from the two women and nodded.

"Hello Asia," he said in a gentle voice.

"Hi Detective Hollis," Asia answered with her head down.

"How are you doing?"

"Okay," she mumbled as her eyes watered.

Asia's tears reminded Ray of the day her son died. He received the call to the barbershop and heard her painful screams before he entered. The remembrance of Asia sitting on the floor rocking her deceased child was difficult, even for him as a veteran officer and detective.

Ray had seen this young woman a hundred times at the courthouse in her cleaning uniform, with her cleaning cart, but he never really looked at her. He sat across from her dumbfounded. *How could I have not seen how pretty she is?* Ray hoped he was not someone who only saw status. He had to admit he never understood the friendship between Patty and Asia. He wondered what they had in common.

"Could I ask you what happened?"

"Yes," she nodded. "I was sitting on the porch when I noticed this guy walking toward the house." She looked down at her lap. "There was something bright in his hand he used to light an object in his other hand. I realized it was a bottle, and it caught fire. He moved the bottle back to throw at Jay's house." She stopped talking and wiped away tears sliding off her cheeks. "I picked up one of the little statues Jay had in her flowerpot and threw it at him. I didn't think---I reacted."

"Asia saved our lives, my little boy Marcus, all of us," Thelma stammered.

"Who's that man, and why'd he want to hurt us?" Asia asked her voice cracking.

"It's not confirmed, I believe it was the man that shot . . ."

"That shot my little boy, is he dead?"

"I don't know, but after I finish talking to you, I'm going to the hospital."

"Hope he's not dead. No mother should have to bury her child," Asia stated before she covered her face with her hands and cried. Thelma embraced her and told her it would be all right.

Ray now understood why Patty cared so much for Asia. *This woman has character.*

Jay slowly walked downstairs and entered the living room. Her blouse tucked halfway in her skirt, and streaks of mascara covered her face. He stood and rushed to her side.

"Are you all right?" he asked.

"Yes, I had to comfort the kids because they were afraid. They're scared a bad man will burn down the house while they're asleep. I'm glad you're here."

Ray saw from Jay's appearance the events of the evening had taken its toll on her, and she was fighting to maintain control. He wished he could take her into his arms and assure her everything would be fine, but he was grateful that she was glad to see him even under the circumstances.

"Did anyone else know you were having this dinner tonight and who the guests would be?"

"It wasn't a secret, but everyone who knew about the party was here tonight."

Ray continued to probe. "Asia and Thelma, could either of you think of anyone you may have told, even if it was in passing?"

Asia and Thelma both shook their heads no.

"We'll have to sort this out, but I believe everyone is safe for right now. Please stay inside the house for a while longer. I'll have a patrol car watch the house for the next few hours. I'm going to the hospital to meet Patty. Maybe, I'll get answers there."

***

As soon as Ray left the house Thelma blurted out, "Shelia knew. I didn't want to say anything until we talked to her."

"How did Sheila know?" Jay asked.

"It was so hot yesterday that I went onto the porch and called the kids to come into the house out of the sun," Thelma said as she stood and paced. "Sheila was on her porch and asked me where you were. I told her at the market getting food for Asia's party and who'd be here, but I didn't believe I'd done anything wrong," she added, stumbling over her words. "It's hard to think Sheila would tell anyone that could be capable of this."

Jay shrugged. "It is."

"Something's different with Sheila," Thelma continued. "She's been acting strange these past couple months. Her phone rang Friday while we were on the porch talking, and she almost broke her neck running into the house to get it. I asked her who had her running as a crazy woman, but she didn't answer me." Thelma resumed pacing. "The call was short, but when she returned to the porch, she appeared distracted."

"Maybe she has a new man she's not ready to introduce to her friends," Asia offered.

"I doubt that very much," Thelma shook her head. "Shelia's an open book and tells it all. She can't hold water. Believe me if she had anybody, she'd have said something. All she talks about is living across the street from a park with no children, and her ticking clock."

"Call and ask her to come over here," Jay requested. "I don't want to leave the kids. You don't think it's too late, do you?"

"Hell, no this is strange, would've expected Shelia to be here by now," Thelma exclaimed. She has to know something happened in here tonight. If nothing else, she should've called."

"Maybe she went out," Asia offered.

Thelma looked through the window at the street, then turned back and said, "If she went out, she left her car."

CHAPTER 25

Sheila reclined on her porch lounge, feeling dejected because she was not invited to Jay's house for the dinner party. She understood the gathering was for Asia's family, Patty, and Thelma came to help, but still she felt left out.

A light illuminated from Jay's house as the door opened and Asia came out and sat on the porch alone. Sheila closed her eyes, wondering why Asia was sitting on the porch during her own party.

She heard a trunk close, opened her eyes, and saw a man with a burning object in his hand about to throw it at Jay's house. She jumped out of her seat when she saw him fall and catch on fire. His screams were the worst sounds she had ever heard. It was a horrible sight as he hollered and rolled around Jay's yard. The burning smell was sickening.

Porch lights came on in front of Jay's home, and Asia's uncle ran toward the man with a rug in his hands. Asia stood on the porch as if she was in a trance, and Thelma came out and took

Asia back into the house. The whole scene was so terrible.

Shortly after the ambulance arrived, there were uniformed police, and other people Sheila could not identify. She heard one police officer tell another he thought the victim was Mad Dog. The mention of Mad Dog was a big blow to her. How could Mad Dog be in Jay's yard with a firebomb in his hand one day after she told Mr. Peck about him? She tried to ignore the feeling in the pit of her stomach when he asked her questions about Asia's going away party.

As the ambulance pulled away, Shelia ran to the toilet to vomit. Her head ached, her stomach felt raw, and she could not stop crying. She sat on the closed toilet seat and buried her head in her hands.

To make matters worse, the cell phone she had gotten from Mr. Peck rang. *What could he want this time of night?* She did not have the desire or strength to talk to him, so she let his call go to voice mail, but he was persistent; he called back several times.

Sheila could not understand why he called numerous times a week and asked if she knew anything concerning Tommie as if her brother's status would change daily.

Mr. Peck was a good listener, and they talked for hours. She told him about her mother, and her wish to go back to school. Sheila confided how she thought she would be married by now and discussed her friends and her brother. However, she did not find out much information on him during their conversations. She knew he and her brother were childhood friends, but neither Mr. Peck nor Tommie shared any details with her.

This whole situation was becoming too much for her to bear. Tommie in jail for murder, and the man who tried to kill her brother was at Jay's house tonight trying to harm her friends. Every time she thought of what could have happened, she felt sick again. Her instincts told her something was not right. She could not get out of her mind she had just told her brother's friend about Mad Dog and Asia's party.

Sheila was on the bathroom floor curled into a ball when she heard the house phone ringing. She lifted her head after realizing Mr. Peck did not have her house phone number. The phone stopped ringing, but started again. She left the bathroom floor and headed for the phone in her bedroom.

"Hello."

"Shelia, why aren't you over here?" Thelma asked. "Don't you know something happened here tonight?"

"I'm sick."

"Sick? I saw you a few hours ago. Are you well enough to come over here? We need to talk to you."

"Can it wait until tomorrow?"

"Have you lost your mind?" Thelma shouted. "We could've been killed tonight! What's wrong with you, don't you care?"

"Uh...I do," Sheila stammered, alarmed by Thelma's response. "Give me five minutes."

"If you are not here in five minutes, I'll be at your front door kicking it down!"

"I'll be there," Shelia, answered knowing she could not postpone facing her friends forever. She went back into the bathroom, brushed her teeth, and put a cold washcloth to her face. She grabbed her house keys and cell phone before leaving to go to Jay's house.

CHAPTER 26

The short walk to Jay's house felt as if it were several miles instead of a few yards. *This must be how it felt to walk the plank on a ship;* Sheila laughed without pleasure. There was the stench of the burning man in the air, and the odor became stronger as she entered Jay's front yard. She could see through the screen door that Jay's front door was open. Someone tried to burn down the house and yet Jay did not close and lock the front door. Sheila entered the house, closed, and locked the door behind her.

"Come in," Jay said as soon as she saw Sheila open the screen door.

Sheila walked in and noticed all eyes were on her.

"We're glad you could make it," Thelma said. "Did you know we could've been killed tonight?"

Sheila's mouth opened, but she could not speak. She felt so guilty.

"Why'd we have to call you to come over here?" Thelma continued to probe.

Forcing herself to answer their questions, Sheila's mouth shook, "I...I...was sitting on my porch when I saw a guy catch on fire in front of the house."

"And you didn't tell anybody what you saw?" Jay asked. "What the hell is wrong with you?"

Sheila took a deep breath, "Asia was standing on the porch. She would know better than me what happened."

"Detective Hollis asked us if we mentioned the party to anyone." Thelma stated, "I told you Friday, right before your cell phone rang, and you almost broke your neck running into the house to answer it."

Sheila opened her mouth to respond but her cell phone rang. *Why did I put this damn phone in my pants pocket?* She remembered how excited she was when she received it in the mail. Mr. Peck told her not to give the cell number to anyone and to keep it with her at all times, in case he called.

"Aren't you going to answer it?" Thelma barked. "Who's calling you this time of night? Or should I say morning!"

Without responding, Sheila retrieved the cell phone from her pocket and turned off the ringer.

"Well," Thelma persisted. "Who in the hell was that blowing up your phone?"

Tears drenched Sheila's face. She opened her mouth, could not speak, and dropped her head.

Asia stood and approached Sheila. "I think you better start talking and you better do it right now!"

Sheila's eyes remained glued to the floor. She had never heard Asia speak with such force, and this made her cry harder. Between muffled tears, she explained, "The phone calls are from a man named Mr. Peck. I've never met him. I talk to him on the phone."

"Who is he?" Thelma asked.

"He's a friend of my brother. They grew up together."

"Brother!" Jay and Thelma shouted.

"You never mentioned you had a brother. We've been neighbors and friends for over three years, and you never once said you had a brother," Thelma remarked.

"So much for the open book theory," Asia said rolling her eyes.

Sheila left the sofa, walked to the buffet in the dining room, and removed a picture of Jay and Kiki. The thought of what could have happened made her feel as if she could be sick again. "My brother, Tommie, sent for me from South Carolina after our mother died. He helped me go to nursing school and buy my house," Sheila said without taking her eyes off Jay and Kiki's picture.

Jay looked at Sheila and frowned. "That still doesn't explain why you never told us about him. What's going on that you didn't tell us you had a brother?"

Sheila returned the picture to the buffet. "My brother didn't want me involved in his business, and we'd meet at locations outside of the city whenever we got together. Tommie didn't want anybody coming at me to get to him."

"What business is your brother in you had to be under cover to see him?" Jay asked.

"You wouldn't understand."

"I would," answered Thelma. "Your brother sounds as if he's involved in criminal activities."

Sheila was silent. Her friends could never understand. While they were going on dates and thinking about parties, she was home in South Carolina caring for her mother. It was a twenty-four-seven job, and the only way she and her mother ate or kept a roof over their heads was from the money her brother sent them.

"My guess is your brother is a dope dealer," Thelma told Sheila. "Am I right?"

"Aren't you being rough?" Jay asked Thelma.

"No, we could've died in here tonight, and what Sheila is saying makes no sense."

"What's going on, Sheila?" Asia asked.

Sheila looked at Asia and cried. "My brother didn't shoot Eric. He's a victim himself," she added between sniffles.

Asia shouted, "What you mean your brother didn't shoot my little boy. Are you telling me the horrible monster outside the barbershop is your brother?"

"My brother's not a horrible monster."

"Maybe *murderer* is a better title!"

"Tommie didn't kill your little boy."

Asia approached Sheila, pointed her finger at her, "If your brother hadn't been there, my baby still be alive. That man was shooting at your brother, and your brother was shooting. How you know he didn't shoot my child?"

"He didn't shoot either Eric or Mr. Joe," Jay said speaking for the first time since the conversation between Asia and Sheila started.

"Jenkins was arrested right after the shootings happened, and he still had his gun on him. The bullets didn't match, and one of the barbers saw Mad Dog shooting. He said Sheila's brother had his back to the shop when he shot back at Mad Dog."

"How's that possible?" Asia asked as she removed her finger from Sheila's face. "When the shooting started, everybody hit the floor. If what he's saying is true why's Patty having Sheila's brother charged with murder?"

"The barber said he was facing the window when it happened, and Patty has her reasons."

"My brother didn't shoot your little boy," Sheila insisted. "The man, who shot your child, laid burning in Jay's front yard. Did his screams make you feel better?" Shelia regretted asking the question as soon as it was out of her mouth.

Asia returned to the sofa, "How could you ask me that question?" Tears drenched her face. "No, hearing that boy's screams and cries didn't make me feel better, but your brother is still responsible for my son's death."

"But he didn't shoot your son."

"Just because your brother didn't shoot my child doesn't mean he's not responsible. His lifestyle made him responsible."

Thelma put her arm around Asia's shoulder. "I know it must be hard..."

"What do you know about hard, Thelma?" Asia screamed through her tears. "You have your boy. Yet, you holler and scream at him."

"This isn't you," Jay said to Asia as she walked over and sat on the opposite side of her friend. "I know you've been through a great deal, but don't lose who you are."

"You're right Jay. I guess I should become a controlled-zombie like you. Not showing any emotion or letting anyone get close, even a man who cares for you," Asia cried.

Jay stood and backed away. "I don't know what you're talking about."

"Yes, you do. There's no way you don't know Ray's in love with you."

"You don't know what you're saying. Ray hasn't shown any interest in me. He hasn't even asked me out on a date."

"I guess not," Asia stated through her tears. "He'd need a blow torch to melt that cold wall you keep around yourself."

"Look, this back and forth is getting us nowhere," Thelma said to Asia. "Believe me tonight opened my eyes to many things I need to work on, but now is not the time to point fingers and criticize each other. We all have our issues, but we could've died in here tonight, and we need to work together to find out what's happening."

Asia dropped her head and spoke in a soft voice, "You're right Thelma, I'm sorry. I don't know why I said those mean things. I'm so hurt and confused. The man who killed my little boy was a boy himself. Before the ambulance came, he was crying for his mother. I can't make sense out of any of this."

Jay nodded. "You're looking for answers where none exist. As hard as it may be to accept, sometimes bad and terrible things happen, but we're your friends, we love you, and we'll help you get through this."

Thelma walked over to Sheila and put her arms around her shoulder. Sheila's small-framed body was shaking. "As hard as this may be, now is the time to come clean concerning your brother and his friend. Someone other than us knew we would be here this evening. Please think if you told anyone about this evening, even if it was just in passing."

"You know I'd never do or say anything to hurt you, Marcus, Kiki, or any of you; but I told Mr. Peck about the party."

"Good Lord, Sheila. How could you?" Asia exclaimed.

Thelma cut her eyes at Asia. "Go on Sheila. What was the conversation?"

"Yesterday when I ran into the house to get the phone, Mr. Peck asked why I took so long to answer." Sheila walked over to the mantle and again picked up the picture of Jay and Kiki. She ran her fingers around the frame and turned around to face her friends. She still did not believe what she told Mr. Peck could have almost gotten her friends killed.

"I told him I was on the porch talking to my next-door neighbor about a going away party Jay was having for Asia. He asked me if I was attending and I told him no, and he asked me who was coming?" Sheila's voice cracked. "I'm sorry; I didn't think I was doing something wrong. I don't think Mr. Peck had anything to do with that man showing up tonight." Shelia did not tell her friends she had given Mad Dog's name to Mr. Peck.

"This still isn't making sense," Jay stated. "Sheila, why were you talking to this man?" How does he know us, and why'd he care if I'm having a party for Asia?"

"My brother gave me his number and told me to call and let Mr. Peck know the attorney he hired visited him. During our talks, I sometimes mentioned you guys. Other than Tommie, you are the only family I have."

"So, that's how your brother was able to retain Murphy. Patty was wondering," Jay said. "What employment does your brother's friend have he could afford to have Sean Lee Murphy represent your brother?"

Sheila shrugged. "I don't know. I never met Mr. Peck in person."

"But your brother knows him," Asia said.

Sheila shrieked, "Tommie had nothing to do with what happened tonight."

"Maybe he didn't," Jay acknowledged. "But if your brother wants to help himself and keep Patty from throwing you under the bus, it may be a good idea for him to tell everything he knows about this Mr. Peck. Was that him on the phone earlier?"

Sheila nodded.

"Call him back," Jay instructed.

"It's one o'clock in the morning."

"I'm sure he'll take your call. Put your phone on speaker so we can hear what he has to say."

Sheila hesitated before she retrieved her phone out of her pocket and called. Her call went to voice mail. She left a message saying she was returning his calls, and there was a situation at her friend's house tonight. Would he please call her back?

"Good," Jay said as she took the phone from Sheila. "I hope he calls back soon. If not, we'll just give the phone to Ray when he returns."

"How do you know the detective will be back soon?" Sheila asked.

"She knows," Asia smiled.

CHAPTER 27

Detective Ray Hollis' head was spinning during the short drive from Jay's house to the hospital. This case was very difficult for him because of the people involved. The thought of what could have happened if Asia had not been on the porch sent chills down his spine.

He pulled into the spot designated for police officers on the hospital parking lot. He got out of the car, and called Patty to ask her to meet him at the elevator on the burn unit floor. Patty agreed to meet him at the elevator and led him into a small office near the waiting area, with a table and two chairs in it. There was an empty desk in the corner with medical supplies with cotton balls, alcohol wipes, gloves, and plastic bags strewn on top of the desk. Ray was glad Patty had secured this small room away from the general waiting room.

"Have you received any news on the suspect's condition, or confirmed his identity?" Ray asked Patty as they entered and closed the door.

"He's still unconscious," Patty, answered as she sat in one of the vacant chairs. "A patrol officer found a wallet in the suspect's car."

"Oh yeah, what's his name?"

"Lamont Tyne is the name on the driver's license but his street name is Mad Dog."

Ray's mouth fell open as he sat on the edge of the chair. "Are you serious? We've been looking everywhere for him."

"I know. The attending physician said he'd give me an update as soon as possible."

"How long should we wait?" Ray asked. "Mad Dog could be out for hours or not wake up at all. This whole thing is so scary and confusing." Ray shook his head in despair. "I don't understand how that boy made it to Jay's house, with every uniformed officer looking for him."

"Makes you realize how precious life is. Maybe it's time you stop tip-toeing around Jay and let her know how you feel."

"Uh...I don't know...what you mean, Patty."

"Stop pretending Ray. It's obvious. Every time she comes in your presence, you turn into a sixteen-year-old boy," Patty laughed. "You face down hardened criminals every day, and you're afraid to ask Jay out on a date."

"Suppose...she says *no*?"

"And suppose she says *yes*?" Patty said patting Ray's hand. "Sometimes you have to take a chance."

"The last time I took a chance was with a nurse I met in this hospital, and that didn't turn out good at all."

"Don't let your past hold you hostage. I bet you were sweating bullets walking through this hospital, afraid you'd walk into your ex-wife," Patty said. "Ray, you have to deal with her because you two have a son together."

"You're right, but enough about me. What about you?"

"What about me?"

"I don't see a man in your life."

"Haven't met the right guy, but when I do, I won't be afraid to let him know."

A loud piercing wail came from the general waiting room. Patty and Ray looked at each other.

He opened the door. "Stay here," he said to Patty as he rushed out of the small office and into the waiting room. A young woman was on the floor, bent over crying and screaming, "You're bastards! You're all bastards!" she shouted while pointing her finger at a uniformed police officer who was approaching her as an older woman struggled to lift her off the floor.

Ray put his hand up to signal to the officer to stop. He approached the woman, and as he got closer, he could see it was Tisha Evans, Mad Dog's mother. He knew her when he worked in patrol. She was a drug user, but harmless.

"Tisha," Ray said with outstretched hands, "You better calm down before you get arrested."

"Don't tell me to calm down. You couldn't catch my son because you're all stupid and ignorant, so you set him up and murder him. I should've known not to trust Foster!" she hollered between tears. **"Once a pig, always a pig, he's, a bastard pig!"**

"What are you talking about Tisha?"

"Like you don't know, you and Foster worked together. I should've known when he gave me that address, it was a set-up," she sobbed.

"Gave you what address?" Ray asked trying to control the tone of his voice.

"Hell, you can stop acting now...mission accomplished. You won, and...killed...my child!" Tisha said as she threw a balled up piece of paper at Ray's chest.

A nurse with the help of the older woman was able to lift Tisha from the floor and led her into a room on the opposite side of the waiting area.

Ray grabbed a tissue from the box on a desk in the waiting area and picked up the paper from the floor. He returned to the room he and Patty occupied and closed the door behind him.

"What's going on?" Patty asked, as soon as Ray entered. "That was Mad Dog's mother. He didn't make it." Ray held the ball of paper in the tissue. "She threw this at me and said Foster delivered it to her."

"Jerome Foster, your ex-partner?"

"Yeah," Ray answered as he put on latex gloves from the box on the desk. He unfolded the wad of paper and laid it on top of the desk. It was a letter-size piece of paper with just one line typed on it.

Patty read aloud, "The main witness and the lead prosecutor will be at 1289 Delair Road tomorrow, Saturday evening between the hours of seven o'clock and approximately nine o'clock. What does this mean?" Patty shrieked. "I know what it states, but how is it possible she got this letter from Foster?"

"I don't know, but believe me I intent to find out," Ray said as he folded the letter and placed it into a plastic bag used for specimen samples.

"Go home Patty and try to get some sleep. I'll check on Jay and catch up with Foster in a few hours."

"Call me as soon as you know something. Don't worry about waking me; I don't think I'll be able to sleep."

"Just promise you'll try to rest," Ray said as he held the door to the room they had been using. "This has been a difficult situation, and it's getting worse by the minute. Where'd you park? I'll walk you to your car."

"I'm in the garage. But before we leave, I want to go downstairs to the emergency room to see if Uncle Mike and Aunt Pearl are still there."

"In the confusion, I forgot about them. I still say he's a good man. It's a shame he got burned, since the boy died anyway."

"You're right, but Uncle Mike would never see it that way."

Patty and Ray rode the elevator to the first floor in silence. Even at this time of the morning, the hospital was busy. Ray was hoping he did not bump into his ex-wife. He realized Patty was right, he needed to communicate better with his ex, for the sake of their son. It was hard to believe how much he and Lena once loved each other. Maybe he was to blame for their marriage failing. Lena told him before they broke up he needed to talk to her more. Maybe he should have talked more, but he did not want to start right now.

CHAPTER 28

Mike and Pearl were at the nurse's station waiting for discharge instructions when Patty and Ray entered the emergency area. Mike had a bandage on his right hand extending to his lower arm.

"Are you all right, Uncle Mike?" Patty asked as she rushed to his side. "What did the doctor say?"

"He has second-degree burns on his hand and wrist," Pearl answered before Mike could. "They want him to stay for observation, but you know how stubborn Mike is. He won't do it, he promises to follow up at the clinic."

"Uncle Mike, maybe you should stay at the hospital overnight to make sure everything is all right."

"Those nurses just want me to stay because I'm so good looking," he laughed.

Pearl pointed her finger at him, "Don't make me send you back in there with a head wound."

"Don't hurt me," Mike said with a chuckle.

Ray smiled at Mike and Pearl. He thought their relationship and marriage was beautiful. Even in times of trouble, they could still laugh together. After this was over, he vowed he would let Jay know how he felt about her.

"How's that boy doing?" Mike asked Patty and Ray.

"He passed Uncle Mike," Patty answered.

Mike shook his head. "What a shame. He was just a kid."

"How can you feel sorry for him?" Ray asked. "He could've killed you and everyone at Jay's house."

"I talk to these kids, and all they know is what they see on the TV. As crazy as it sounds, it may not have dawned on him that someone could die."

Patty rolled her eyes. "Come on Uncle Mike, no one's that stupid."

"Yes, they are, as I was putting out that fire, I heard that kid crying and praying for his mother. Those are not the actions of a hard, cold-hearted killer."

"God took him home, and I'm tired," Pearl commented to her husband. "Plus you need rest, so let's get you home."

An attractive, serious-looking nurse came from the examination area with papers in her hand. She took a few steps, and stopped before she approached Mike.

"Mr. Wallace, here are your prescriptions and release instructions with a number for you to call to schedule your appointment at the clinic."

"Thank you," Pearl said as she retrieved the paperwork from the nurse.

"Take care." She turned and said, "Hi Patty," before continuing to leave.

"Lena," Ray called. "Please wait. Can I talk to you?" Ray said as he took a few steps to catch up with her.

"I'm working Ray," she snapped. "And I don't have time for any foolishness."

"I won't take much of your time. I want to ask how you're doing."

"Why do you care?" She asked turning to face him.

"I care because you are the mother of my child, and a good person. I care because I want you to be happy, you deserve to be happy." Ray saw the surprised look on Lena's face. He took her silence as an opportunity and continued. "Tonight reminded me that anyone's life could be cut short at a moment's notice. That man you gave discharge papers to was burnt trying to help a young man that could've killed him, his wife, Patty, and other innocent people."

Lena looked over at Mike, Patty, and Pearl with her mouth open. Then she redirected her gaze at Ray.

"I've spent most of my life trying to avoid personal conflict, even to the point I didn't let you know how much I loved you. I know it's too late for us, but we still have Ray, Jr. Maybe we can be civil for his sake and one day maybe friends again." Ray could not determine what Lena was thinking as she stood there. He hoped he had not crossed the line.

"That would be very nice," she said. "This weekend when you pick up Ray Jr. come to my house instead of going to my mother's house," she instructed before smiling and walking away.

Ray grinned, nodded his head, and turned to walk back to Patty, Pearl, and Mike. They were watching him as he returned.

"Good work," Patty said.

"Yeah," Mike added. "Remember, when a woman's happy, you have sunshine; but when she's not, you've got torrential rain."

"Mike, behave. Let's go home." Pearl said.

"Don't forget Pearl," Mike stated. "We have to get Asia."

"You two go on home," Ray said. "I have to go by Jay's house, so I'll bring Asia home if she isn't asleep."

"Thank you Detective Hollis," Mike said as Pearl nodded.

"You're welcome and call me Ray. I'll contact you both later."

CHAPTER 29

Ray parked in front of Jay's house and sat in his car, wondering if it was too early in the morning to knock on her door. He sat for a few minutes and decided he would tap on the door and come back later if there was no answer. He got out of his car, knocked lightly, and Jay opened the door right away.

"Hello," she said with a broad smile as she swung the door open. "Thanks for returning so soon."

He entered the living room, and noticed Asia curled up, asleep in a chair. Across from her, Thelma was on one end of the couch and Shelia on the other; both were asleep.

Jay took Ray's hand, led him into the kitchen, and closed the door. "Would you like some tea?" she asked as she placed a teapot on the stove. "I'm having a cup."

"Yes, thanks. I see everybody's asleep."

"They're tired. There was a bunch of drama in here after you left last night."

"What happened?" Ray asked giving Jay an inquiring look.

"Nothing too serious, a little name calling. Let me fix some tea," Jay said as she retrieved two cups and saucers from the cupboard and placed a tea bag in each of the cups. She grabbed Shelia's cell phone, and placed it in front of Ray.

He picked up the phone and examined the features. "Nice this just came out and is small, not big as that brick I have. Whose phone is it?"

"It belongs to Sheila. She got it from her brother's childhood friend, so they could keep in touch regarding her brother's situation."

"Who's her brother?"

"Thomas Jenkins."

Ray frowned. "Are you talking about the same Thomas Jenkins involved in the shooting?"

"None other," Jay answered. "No one knew she had a brother, much less he was involved in Eric's death."

"This is not good."

"It gets worst. This childhood friend was the one who hired Sean Lee Murphy to represent her brother."

"That mystery's solved."

"Here's the real kicker, Shelia told this friend about the dinner party last night, including the names of everyone who'd be here."

"What!"

Jay reached over and took the teapot off the stove before the whistling disturbed anyone in the next room. "You take one sugar?"

"Yes," Ray smiled as he realized Jay had been paying enough attention to him to know how many sugars he took in his tea. "Why did she give him that information? And for crying out loud, who's this childhood friend?"

"Sheila was running her mouth when she gave out the information on the party," Jay said as she handed Ray his tea. "Believe it or not, she doesn't know who this friend is and calls him Mr. Peck, but she never met him or seen a picture of him."

"This gets worse and worse," Ray said, as he picked up the cell phone and examined it again.

"We had her call him back a few times after he left her several messages, but the calls went to voice mail." Jay said taking a sip of her tea.

"What are you guys, junior detectives? What would you have done if he answered the phone?"

"We hadn't gotten that far," Jay admitted.

"I told Patty to get some rest, but I'll need to call and wake her up if she's asleep." Ray shook his head and placed the cell phone on the table.

"Don't worry. I doubt if she's asleep."

Ray called Patty, and she answered on the first ring.

"I hope it's not a bad time, but we need to talk."

"What's up?"

Ray gave Patty complete information about Thomas Jenkins, Sheila being his sister, Jenkins childhood friend, and the cell phone.

Patty sighed, "Do you have the cell phone?"

"Yeah, our junior detectives had Sheila call him, but the calls went to voice mail."

"Unbelievable."

"Here's the problem, I'm sure we could find out where the phone was purchased and who the service provider is, but the phone was more than likely purchased under a false name."

"What about getting it cloned?" Patty asked. "Then we could hear their conversations."

"We'd have to go to the feds to get it cloned."

"Forget that. I'm not turning this case over to the feds."

"Patty, if Jenkins is charged with murder in furtherance of a drug transaction, the penalties would be tougher if we turned this case over to the feds."

"Yeah that's true, but maybe we don't have to take that route. The mere mention of turning this case over to the feds could have Murphy encouraging his client to cooperate and give us information about his childhood friend."

Patty paused and exhaled. "Hell, if that don't work, we can use his baby-sister Shelia, as bait. I'm sure he wouldn't want her to go to jail."

"But she hasn't done anything wrong," Ray countered, not wanting to arrest Sheila.

"We can hold her for questioning."

Ray nodded in agreement. "You work on that angle with Murphy, and soon I'll call Foster to find out how Tisha got Jay's address. Between the two of us, maybe we can make sense out of this craziness."

"Okay, I'll call you soon as I can to give you an update."

Ray disconnected the call with Patty and turned to Jay, "Is it's all right with you if I stayed here for a few hours until it's time to call Foster?"

"Sure, do you want to go upstairs to my bedroom to rest?"

Ray thought of how he would love to go to Jay's bedroom, but not now and not without her. He shook his head no, "I'll sit here if you don't mind. I need a moment to chill."

"Of course it's all right. You don't need to ask."

CHAPTER 30

We must have fallen asleep; and are still in the hospital, Tisha thought as she heard the sound of screeching wheels. She left the sofa, peeped through the door entry, and spotted a nurse pushing a hospital cart. Tisha wondered if the nurse that brought them to this room forgot and went home.

The sun shone through the blinds and landed on her mother sleeping in a chair in the corner of the room. She watched her mother's chest move in a rhythmic pattern. Macy was once a beautiful woman. There were still remnants of her beauty remaining, but life had taken a toll on her aging body. Tisha continued watching her mother and admitted Macy was more of a mother to Lamont than she was, his death had to be difficult for her mother.

They lived in the house Macy's father left after he died. Twenty-five years earlier when he purchased the house, the neighborhood had working-class residences who took pride in their community. Their neighborhood was now one of the worst crime and drug-infested areas in west Baltimore.

Tisha saw her mother attempt to protect Lamont. She took him to church and Sunday school. They went to the movies, museums, and plays. She signed him up for the Boy Scouts, karate, and music lessons, but every time he left the house, the streets beckoned him with the lure of fast and easy money, and excitement. In addition, Tisha knew Lamont sold drugs to support her habit, and she felt guilty about her son's death. Foster told her hurtful but true things.

She felt sick: had a headache, was feeling nauseated and her joints ached. Tisha knew what was happening to her and welcomed the pain---punishment for the mistakes she made with her mother and son.

Macy sat up in the chair and looked at her daughter. "Are you okay?"

Tisha's eyes watered. "Yes, I guess so," she sobbed.

"No, you're not. You're in pain. I can handle things here if you need to leave."

"I can't do this anymore, Mommy," Tisha said wiping her nose. "This is why my baby is gone."

"I'm hurting too, but beating yourself up will not bring Lamont back."

"I have to get help."

"We're in a hospital," Macy said as she left her seat and walked over to Tisha. "If you're serious about getting help, we can go downstairs to the emergency room."

"Mommy, can you help me?" Tisha cried holding her arms out to her mother.

"Yes baby, I'm here for you," Macy said holding her daughter in her arms.

She held onto her mother as they left the room and made their way to the elevator. Macy pushed the button to the first floor as they rode in silence. The hospital was busy; but Tisha felt invisible. They reached the first floor, and Macy put her arm around her daughter's slender waist as she guided her down a long hall leading to the emergency room.

Tisha's walk slowed as they approached the front entrance of the hospital, several feet from the emergency room reception area. She wanted to run out the front entrance and catch a cab to where she could find something or somebody to end her pain, but she looked into her mother's face and saw hope. Tisha could not believe her mother still had hope. Macy half-carrying Tisha tightened her arm around her daughter's slim waist and Tisha felt stronger.

Making it past the front entrance, caused Tisha to remember the times Lamont had gotten her into several treatment programs. She never completed any of the programs. She had been down this road before. Her heart ached as she thought Lamont might still be alive if she had. Tisha felt overwhelmed with guilt, shame, and grief, and had difficulty breathing.

"Hold on precious, we're almost there."

"I know Mommy, I'm good."

They continued to walk with Tisha leaning on Macy for support. No one approached them or asked if they needed any help. The medical staff walked around them without a second look or glance.

Tisha stopped walking as soon as they made it to the emergency room sign. She wondered if going to the emergency room was a good idea. Maybe she should try to get clean on her own. She knew she was just fooling; she could never get thru detox by herself. Her son died a horrible death, and she had to do this for him.

"We'll almost there. Just be strong." Macy urged, gently pushing her daughter forward. "Oh my goodness, there's Debra, your cousin," Macy said as they entered the emergency room check-in area.

Debra left her desk, walked over to Tisha and Macy, and threw her arms around the two of them. "I was here when they brought Lamont in," she said to them. "I'm so sorry. He was unconscious and the nurse in the burn unit told me he never regained consciousness. When he left here, he was not in pain. I've been praying for you," she said as she took Tisha's hand.

"Thank you," Macy said as Tisha nodded her head.

"Is there any way Tisha could see a doctor for her..."

"Flu symptoms," Debra said cutting Macy off as she walked back to her desk and picked up a clipboard with papers on it. "Fill out these forms as best you can."

"Tisha," Macy asked, "Are you going to be okay? I need to go back upstairs to see what arrangements we have to make for Lamont."

"Go ahead Aunt Macy," Debra responded. "I'll be off in an hour, but if you are not back by them, I'll stay here with her until you return."

Tisha began filling out the forms, but her hands shook, and Debra took the clipboard and completed the forms for her, asking Tisha questions when she got to an item she could not answer.

The forms completed, Tisha went into the waiting room and listened for her name. She found an empty chair, sat back, and closed her eyes. Her body began screaming at her and she was hurting. Feeling helpless and alone, Tisha did something she had not done since she was a child---she prayed.

CHAPTER 31

Morning sunbeams shone through Jay's kitchen windows and acted as a wake-up call. Ray lifted his head from a pillow and gazed at Jay who was resting her head on her arms. He knew Jay had to be the one to slide the pillow under him, but he did not know when she did it. She could have gone to her bedroom, but he was glad she stayed. He thought again, how much he cared for her, and what a wonderful person she was.

Ray opened the kitchen door, browsed the living room, and saw everyone was still asleep. The house was quiet except for the ticking clock on the kitchen wall. It was seven o'clock in the morning. He watched as Jay lifted her head from the kitchen table and smiled.

"Good morning, beautiful. Do you always wake up smiling?"

Jay blushed. "You want a cup of coffee?"

"No. But could I talk to you?" He reached across the table and held out his hand to her. Jay placed her hand in his.

Ray took a deep breath, "I care for you. I have for some time, but I've been afraid to tell or let you know."

"Why?"

"That's a good question. I was afraid I wasn't the man you'd want, and that you'd think I was silly for even approaching you. I was afraid you'd reject me."

"You don't know how long I've been waiting for you to show an interest in me." Jay lightly squeezed Ray's hand, looked into his eyes, and smiled.

"It took this tragedy for me to muster the courage," Ray said shaking his head. "My timing may not be the best, but maybe when this ordeal is over, we can go to a movie, or dinner, or both."

"What a great idea. I'm ready whenever you are."

"I need a few days to make sure everybody is safe...and can I use your bathroom," Ray said as he stood up and chuckled. Jay smiled and shook her head.

Ray walked through the living room trying not to disturb the women. He wanted to dance and sing as he went up to the second floor. The bathroom was sparkling clean. He believed you could tell a good deal about a woman by how she kept her home.

He returned downstairs, and the kids were watching cartoons, Thelma and Jay were in the kitchen preparing breakfast, and Asia was sitting at the kitchen table drinking coffee. Shelia was on the end of the sofa with her eyes closed, but he knew there was no way she could be asleep with all this activity.

Even when his son was with him, his home life was tame compared to Jay's house with her friends and family. He realized if he wanted to be with Jay, he would have to accept her child, and her friends.

Ray sat in the chair across from Sheila and tapped her on the shoulder. Sheila opened her eyes, and he asked her to come out on the porch and talk to him. She stood and followed him. She looked so sad he felt sorry for her.

"Sheila, please tell me everything about your conversations with Mr. Peck?" Ray asked as he pulled her cell phone from his pocket.

Her bottom lip quivered as she gave detailed information about her brother's friend. "I don't think Mr. Peck had anything to do with what happened here last night."

Ray wrote notes on a small writing pad he retrieved from his jacket pocket. He turned to Sheila, "Did you tell Mr. Peck that Mad Dog was the person who tried to kill your brother?"

Sheila stood silent as tears rolled down her face. "Yes," she admitted.

Ray sat on Jay's porch and wondered what to do with the information Sheila provided. "You keep this cell phone for right now. If you get any calls from Mr. Peck, talk normal, and call me as soon as he hangs up." Ray examined the phone again before giving it to Sheila.

"If he calls, what should I say to him?"

"Tell him what happened at Jay's house as he will probably know, and talk normal."

"Are you going to arrest me?"

"No, but I can't make you any promises. Your cooperation in helping us solve this case could keep you out of jail. That's why I need you to stay in contact with Mr. Peck."

"You can count on me."

"Thank you," Asia, Thelma, and Jay uttered.

Ray turned around and the three women were standing in the door entrance. He did not hear them come to the door and wondered how long they had been standing there. He laughed despite himself. Last night the women were at each other throats, but today they were a unified force. Shaking his head, he wondered if he would ever understand women.

***

Ray took Asia home on his way to meet Foster. Sheila went home and Thelma took Marcus and Kiki with her. Jay was alone with her thoughts. She was thankful no one was seriously injured or killed last night. Jay wondered how long it would have taken Ray to talk to her if that boy had not tried to light a bottle filled with gasoline and throw it at her house.

No matter the reason, she was glad he got the courage. She admired Ray's calm strength. He did not lose his cool, even when dealing with Patty, who could be aggressive. Jay closed her eyes and fantasized about getting lost in the dimples in Ray's handsome cocoa-colored face, and his tall, slim, strong body sparked the fire in her heart and her body that had been still for so long.

Asia told her about the cold wall she built, and she had to admit Asia was right. "That wall will be coming down," she said looking at her reflecting in the mirror on the dining room wall. "That wall is coming down," she repeated.

CHAPTER 32

Jerome's eyes flew wide open to the sound of the phone ringing on his nightstand. He wanted to ignore the call but was curious to know who was calling him so early on a Sunday morning. He glanced at his wife, who was still asleep, before he turned on the lamp and looked at the caller ID.

Frowning, Jerome wondered why Ray Hollis was calling. He had not heard from Ray since retiring from the police force. He picked up the phone from its cradle, "Good morning, Ray," he said in a low voice, "What's going on?"

"We need to talk."

"Why?"

"I'll explain everything when we meet in person."

"Meet me at my office in hour," he told Ray since his office was not open on Sunday.

Jerome grimaced after he hung up the phone and noticed his wife was still sleeping peacefully. He smiled looking at her and thought what a wonderful evening they had last night. It was the first time they had gone out since he started his new business. They went to dinner at the Prime Steak restaurant for dinner, and after dinner, they went dancing at the Ninth Mile, a nightclub owned by an ex-police friend, who treated them as royalty.

Dana looked beautiful, sexy, and classy. His wife could teach young women how to look sexy without looking trashy. Jerome felt on top of the world as he could see the admiration and envy in the eyes of several men in the club.

They ended the great evening with the best lovemaking they had made in several months. He needed last night---attempting to hold his business together, fearing he would lose his home, and trying to keep his trouble a secret from his wife. Jerome did not know what was going on, but promised not to let Ray bring him down from this good feeling.

He quietly climbed out of bed without waking his wife and dressed to meet Ray at his office. They had worked together for several years, but never formed a bond. Ray was too straight for Jerome's taste. The job of being a police was too stressful not to have a release, and he did not trust a police officer who had no vices.

Jerome returned to the office on Friday after delivering the letter to Tisha and received a call from his newest client. Brian Adams asked Jerome to overnight the receipt. Completing that task, Jerome went online and noticed there was another three-thousand dollars deposited in his bank account, and he transferred the money to pay as many bills as he could. He knew there was something wrong with how the money appeared in his account, but he did not want to make an issue of how it got there because he did not want to give it back.

Jerome arrived at the parking space in front of his office and noticed Ray sitting there waiting for him.

"Thanks for meeting me," Ray said as he greeted Jerome with a handshake.

"Follow me," Jerome said. He unlocked his office door and led Ray through the reception room to his office. "Have a seat," Jerome said as he sat behind his desk and pointed to the chair across from his desk.

Ray sat in the chair and leaned forward. "I suppose you want to know why I called this meeting," he said as he reached into his pocket, pulled out the one-page letter he received from Tisha, and showed it to Jerome.

Jerome read it, and returned the letter to Ray. "What does this letter have to do with me?"

"Tisha said she got it from you."

"What! I've never seen this note before, and I know you didn't wake me up this morning based on what that junkie said. I don't know what this means. Who are the main witness and lead prosecutor? And who lives at 1289 Delair Road?"

"I'm hoping you can tell me why Tisha said she got this letter from you?"

"What...are...you accusing me of, Ray?"

"I'm not accusing you. I'm just asking you to answer a simple question."

"Sounds like an accusation."

Ray sat back in his chair and told Jerome everything that happened last night. After he stopped talking, neither of the men spoke for several seconds. The only sound in the room was the ticking of the clock Jerome received as a retirement gift. He never realized how loudly it ticked until now and wondered why people gave clocks and watches as retirement gifts. Shouldn't retirement mean you are less concerned with time?

Jerome sat there struggling with how much to tell Ray about the envelope he had delivered to Tisha on Friday. He liked Patty and going after an assistant state's attorney was the same as going after a police officer.

He exhaled and said, "I'm sorry about what happened last night, but I'm telling you the truth when I say, I never saw that letter. I shouldn't be telling you this, but I delivered a small envelope to Tisha at Pee Wee's on Friday afternoon. My client instructed me not to open the envelope. I gave it to Tisha, she signed for it, and I left and didn't see what was in the envelope."

"Who's your client?"

"Come on Ray, I can't tell you that. If I reveal my clients, I just as well close my door because no one will hire or trust me."

"Trust you? What about your obligation to do the right thing?" Ray leaned on the edge of the desk. "Your client may be responsible for almost getting people I care about killed. Not to mention, he may also have a part to play in Mad Dog's death."

Jerome frowned. "Oh, so now you care about Lamont. Don't run that game on me."

"That was a terrible way for anyone to die, even a low life like Mad Dog."

"You didn't know him, Mr. Perfect so don't pass judgment on him."

"You're so right, I didn't know Lamont, but being burned to death is not the way I'd want to go. Listen Jerome, this back and forth is getting us nowhere. I need your help."

Jerome sat back in his chair. He could not believe Ray's nerve. Whenever he invited Ray out after work to have a drink, he was always too busy. *Now, he sits in my office saying he needs my help.*

"Will you help me?" Ray asked interrupting Jerome's thoughts.

"I did nothing wrong Jerome explained in his defense. "Even though, I didn't know what was in the envelope, I knew it was not drugs or any illegal substances."

"Man, you were a police officer for twenty-five years, and delivering that letter to Tisha could not have felt right. You can't tell me you didn't believe someone hiring you to deliver a letter to the mother of Mad Dog, who shot one person, killed an innocent child, and who the entire department was trying to find was not strange?"

Jerome left his desk and walked over to his coffee machine. He kept his back to Ray because he did not want Ray to see he had touched a nerve. In addition to accepting the money, the other thing he did wrong was helping Lamont because of Macy. There were times Jerome had asked arresting officers not to report the true amount of drugs Lamont had when arrested. If he had not, Lamont could be in jail, instead of dead.

He poured water in the container and added the coffee into the filter. While it was brewing, Jerome prepared himself to face his ex-partner. He returned to his desk and spoke to Ray in an even tone.

"Despite what you say Ray, I can't reveal the identity of my client, but I will tell you he called me Friday evening after I delivered the envelope to Tisha. After he hung up, I hit star sixty-nine, and a man answered the phone telling me I had called a coffee shop in Boston."

"Boston? Are you telling me the person who hired you lives in Boston?"

"No, I'm telling you that the individual who hired me, called me from a coffee shop in Back Lake, Boston."

"Back Lake is an upscale section in Boston. Why'd anyone call you from there? Every time I open one door in this case, it leads me down a long hall to another." Ray shook his head before asking, "Do you have the name of the shop?"

"No, I don't"

"Is the number still on your phone?"

"No, once another call comes in, the previous number is erased. I'm sorry I couldn't be of more assistance to you. I really like Patty, and I'm glad no one at her assistant's house was seriously injured or killed." Jerome stood up and walked over to his office door, knowing he had lied, as another call had not come in, but knew he had to give Ray something.

"I appreciate your help," Ray said as he stood to leave.

Jerome directed his ex-partner through the reception room and toward the front door. After Ray left, Jerome returned to his office, closed the door, and buried his head in his hands.

***

Dana still basting in the magnificent love she and her husband made last night saw the note he left on her pillow---*Loved last night, went to meet Ray Hollis*. She wondered if Jerome's meeting with Ray had anything to do with what was troubling her husband the last few months. Dana thought he would enjoy retirement, away from the crimes he investigated as a patrol officer and homicide detective.

She was surprised when he first talked of opening an investigation business and wondered why he did not want to do something easier.

Operating a business was hard work, especially in the beginning years. She appreciated Jerome giving Sayda a job. She knew the two of them did not care for each other. Now they were working together, she hoped her daughter and husband could form a close bond.

CHAPTER 33

Glenn replaced his cell phone in the charger after listening to Sheila's messages. He did not return her calls; the change in her behavior was a red flag to him. She never talked before with the speaker on, and her voice sounded different. *Something is up with her,* he thought as he sat back in his chair and clasped his hands behind his head.

This moment reminded him of the times he lived with the Pecks. He learned to read Mary out of a sense of protection. She was never nice to him but on certain days, she was more brutal than usual. He became efficient in reading her moods and on her bad days, he did his best to stay out of her way.

He guarded himself as an adult because he had too many secrets and avoided situations that opened the door for people to ask questions of his personal life and background. Winston was the only person he associated with outside of business, and his friend was too busy whining about his own life to pry or ask Glenn personal questions. Only Tommie and maybe Aunt Pearl knew his childhood secret. Glenn had time to think of how to handle Tommie. Under the very best of circumstances, even with Murphy as his lawyer, Tommie was on his way to jail.

His Aunt Pearl was the immediate concern. When Glenn met her at Winston's house, he suspected she knew he was her nephew. He believed she would not want to hurt him on purpose, but a few questions could start people wondering about him.

Sitting back in his bedroom with a glass and a bottle of wine, he remembered William Bolt, Priscilla's father, arranging a late-night meeting between them in his private study away from the ears of his servants. Glenn entered the home that night with a code Bolt had given him and went directly upstairs to the private room.

William Bolt had investigated his daughter's suitor and found out that Glenn had deceived Priscilla. Nothing Glenn had told her was true. He was not from Philadelphia, his family never had a dry cleaning establishment, and he was born to a poor black teenager in an obscured place in South Carolina. Bolt offered Glenn a check of two hundred-thousand dollars to leave and never return. In exchange, he would spare Glenn the embarrassment of being exposure to Priscilla as a fraud.

Glenn accepted Bolt's officer, and after the meeting, they were at the top of the staircase. Bolt had a smirk on his face as he reached out to shake hands. The brakes on his wheelchair had not been set, and the chair began sliding over the edge of the landing. Glenn could have stopped it, but instead moved aside and let Bolt and the chair roll down the steps.

The next day, Glenn received a call from Priscilla very distraught telling him her father had an accident, fell down the stairs, and was dead. Glenn destroyed the check, and he and Priscilla married two months later.

Continuing to drink his wine, he listened to the late night national news; and heard the reporter state a suspect burned in Baltimore City trying to throw a firebomb at a house with a witness in it against him and later died.

Glenn realized the suspect was Mag Dog. He was not sure what Mad Dog would do with the information Foster delivered to the mother. He hoped Mad Dog could do enough damage to take Aunt Pearl's mind off him---throw a rock through the window with a note, shoot at the house, or write a warning on the front door. Never in a million years, did he believe Mad Dog would have died.

He did not view Foster as a problem. The private investigator did not know that Brian Adams and Glenn Peck was the same person. He preferred no one else died, but could accept that possibility if it kept the focus off him.

Gulping another glass of wine, he walked over to his closet door, and opened it. He searched the back on his walk-in closet and retrieved his box with the photograph of his mother, Aunt Pearl, and himself. No one was around to see it; but he still kept it hidden there.

Glenn reclined in his leather chair staring at the picture, listening to music, drinking his wine, and wondering what to do next. He watched the sun come up and knew time was against him. Whatever he did, it needed to be soon.

He poured the last of the bottle into his glass and took it downstairs to his study. At his desk, he turned on his computer, and searched for information on homes in west Baltimore. He discovered many of the residents lived in row homes built in the late eighteen hundreds through early nineteen hundreds. In those days, many of the homes had coal furnaces, which were later converted to oil for heating and gas for cooking.

From the information he learned on the houses in Baltimore, he developed a plan of how to take care of Aunt Pearl. He wondered how to get to Baltimore fast and not raise questions. He could book a commercial flight, but that might leave a paper trail, and it took too long to drive there, or go by train. Glenn decided there might be fewer questions if he took his company's plane, since he had a pilot's license and had flown the plane. It was Sunday and less people than normal were at the plane hangar at the private airport. He would worry about what to put on the flight logs later, and he could rent a van once he arrived in Baltimore.

His head was swimming as Glenn mapped out his plans. As an afterthought, he went back upstairs and entered his wife's bedroom for the first time since she died. He opened the chest at the foot of her bed, removed the gun case, and took out her handgun. He had gone to the shooting range with his wife on numerous occasions and was comfortable handling guns, even though he did not like them.

Returning to his bedroom, he searched his closet for dark pants, shirt, shoes, baseball cap, and black sneakers. He decided he could get the rest of the supplies he needed once he arrived in Baltimore. He pulled out an overnight bag and placed into it, the gun, and the items he had removed from his closet.

Glenn stopped packing and stared at his image in the mirror. "Are you seriously prepared to do this?" he asked his reflection. *Maybe I'm approaching this all wrong.* He thought about calling his aunt since he should not have much trouble finding her phone number. He could tell her who he was, explain to her the life he now had, and tell her he did not want to jeopardize what he had accomplished. He could let her know there were people who may challenge his position if they knew he was a different person than he portrayed. The real question was could he trust her to keep his identity a secret, considering she had been looking for him for thirty years.

I have no choice Glenn thought as he went into the bathroom, took a shower, dressed, and headed to the airport.

CHAPTER 34

Ray sat in his car on the parking lot outside of Jerome's business trying to make sense of the information he had received and wondered if his ex-partner, Foster, was withholding more than his client's name. Ray's stomach was growling, and he realized he had not eaten since yesterday afternoon. He was trying to decide which fast food place was closest when his cell phone rang.

"What's going on?" he asked Patty.

"I've arranged a meeting with Murphy and his client, Jenkins, at the pre-trial center at one o'clock this afternoon. Can you make it?"

"Yeah, I can make it," he said after checking his watch.

"Good. I'll meet you there."

He snickered realizing Patty likely used a private number to reach the attorney on an early Sunday morning. He was sure Patty pressured the attorney to get him to agree to a meeting under such short notice. Ray suspected Patty and Murphy had dated in the past because they were so edgy in one another's presence, but Patty never volunteered that tidbit of information and Ray never asked. It reminded him of the way he and his ex-wife acted, but on a smaller scale.

Ray cared for and respected Patty, but never underestimated her. She was an interesting and complex person, who could be forceful, or thoughtful and sensitive. He would have paid good money to hear the conversation between Murphy and Patty.

Checking his watch again, Ray surmised he had time to get something to eat, go home to shower, and change. He disliked going to the center. The place made him cringe. It was dark, dirty, and dismal; and Ray always felt something was crawling on him when he left there.

He hated to see the older people that came to see their loved ones, especially the women, grandmothers he presumed. Many of them were on canes, walkers, and even in wheel chairs, with no special accommodations made for them. They waited in long lines to enter the building in the bitter cold or blazing heat as everyone else.

Ray felt bad for the grandparents, who were raising many young people. He saw the same thing in court. It was the grandparents paying bails and putting up their homes for a bunch of ungrateful kids.

He started the ignition and looked at the front window of Jerome's office. As he put his car in reverse and backed out of the parking lot, he wondered if Jerome was waiting for him to pull off, before exiting.

CHAPTER 35

Glenn flew the Thrifty Bank owned Cessna-172 from Boston to Martin State Airport. It was the first time he traveled to Baltimore without his late wife, and there was always a limousine and a driver waiting for them.

After renting a van, he entered the small airport. Inside was a gift shop containing cards, plants, and balloons. He picked out the biggest and most beautiful of the plants for purchase. Carrying the plant to the checkout counter, he saw a section with maps, and selected a map of Baltimore. He checked with the cashier as he paid for his items and found his destination was some thirty to forty minutes from the airport.

Glenn reviewed his list to ensure he had everything he needed before he pulled off the airport lot---his gun, a wrench set, two rolls of duct tape from the hangar in Boston, a map of the Baltimore metropolitan area, and the plant. His list was complete. Glenn put his equipment into the van and changed into the items he had in his overnight bag.

He rehearsed his plan several times in his head during the ride to his destination. He tried to think of another way to make sure Aunt Pearl did not interfere with his life, but he could not come up with a better idea. He would have to suck it up and follow his present strategy; there was no other way Glenn kept telling himself.

His heart was pumping as he parked his van in front of Sheila's house. He had retained her address from when he sent her the cell phone. Glenn liked Sheila even though he had not met her in person and often used Tommie as an excuse to call her. They would talk on the phone for hours. She was very talkative, friendly, and inviting every time they spoke. She made him realize how lonely he was. He told himself not to get too involved with her because she could never fit into his world, and he may have to destroy hers.

Glenn left the driver's seat, opened the rear side door, and discreetly removed his gun and slid it into his pants pocket. He retrieved the large plant, shut the door, walked from the curb to Sheila's house, and rang her doorbell.

After a few seconds, a young pretty woman answered the door, and Glenn announced a delivery for Shelia Jenkins as she shrieked with delight. He recognized her voice from their many conversations. Shelia opened the door; Glenn shoved her with the plant and pushed his way inside her house. He entered pulling out his gun. "Don't scream or try to run," he warned in the most menacing voice he could muster. He could see the fear on her face and regretted he had to threaten her. Despite himself, Glenn found her refreshing.

She looked so frightened, her slender body shook, and tears fell from her big brown eyes.

Sheila whimpered, "I don't have very much money, but you can have what I've got. Please don't hurt me," she pleaded with trembling lips.

"I won't hurt you Sheila, but I need you to cooperate with me."

Sheila froze in place upon hearing Glenn call her name. "Your voice... Mr. Peck?"

"Yes, and I won't hurt you if you cooperate."

"Why did you force your way into my home, and why are you pointing a gun at me?" she cried.

"Calm down Sheila. I won't hurt you if you do as I say."

"What do you want, Mr. Peck?"

"I need you to take me to Asia's house."

"Why?"

"I don't have time for your questions. I won't hurt you unless you force me," Glenn said as he pointed his gun at Sheila.

"Are you going to hurt Asia?" When he did not respond, she asked, "Did you send Mag Dog to burn down Jay's house?"

"No more questions Sheila. We need to leave right now. Pick up the plant."

Sheila bent over and recovered the plant that fell when Glenn forced his way into her home and tried to scoop the dirt that spilled on the floor.

"Leave the dirt. We don't have time for that," Glenn barked, thinking the dirt on the floor was the least of her problems.

He pushed Sheila out the door and instructed her to walk to the van parked in front of her house. She carried the plant, and Glenn walked behind her with his gun pressed in her back. He opened the side door, and told Sheila to put the plant on the floor of the van. Closing the door, he pointed to the passenger's seat and ordered her to get inside the van.

Sheila would not move. "I'm not going," she insisted. "I've done enough to hurt Asia, and I'm not taking you to her house."

"Don't you realize I have a gun? I will shoot you if you make me."

Glenn reached around Sheila, opened the door, and shoved her into the front passenger seat. "Stop crying," he grumbled. "Fasten your seat belt and don't try anything stupid. I can shoot faster than you can run."

***

Thelma was at her second floor bedroom window checking on Marcus and Kiki playing in the park when she saw a deliveryman get out of a van with a large beautiful plant and take it into Sheila's house. She stayed at the window waiting for him to leave so she could run over and find out who sent the plant.

203

While waiting, Thelma saw Sheila come out of her house carrying the plant and the man walking closely behind her. He shoved Sheila into the passenger's side of a van. Thelma ran down the steps from her bedroom to her porch, but by the time she made it, the van was gone. She ran as fast as she could to Jay's house, banging on the door until Jay answered. "I think Sheila's been kidnapped," she shouted at the top of her lungs.

"How do you know?"

Thelma told Jay how a deliveryman brought a plant to Sheila's house and shoved her into a van.

"Oh my God! Did you get the tag number?"

"No, by the time I realized something was wrong, they had gone," Thelma cried. "Maybe we should call the police?"

"They'll take too long and ask a million questions. I'll call Ray and Patty. They'll know what to do."

CHAPTER 36

Tommie was sitting on a cot in his cell when he heard his name called for an attorney visit. He had been locked-up for two months and seen his attorney once. Sean Lee Murphy was known as being the best criminal attorney in the city; however, Tommie was not impressed with him

The guard took the handcuffs off, and Tommie entered a cold, windowless room to meet his lawyer. Sporting a golf shirt, hat, and pants, Murphy looked as if someone dragged him off a golf course. Tommie noted his attorney sitting at a small table with folded arms and a scowl on his face, and pulled out a chair and sat on the opposite side of the table.

"What's going on?" Tommie asked. "You've only visited me once in two months and here you come dressed as if you are going to a damn golf course."

"We have a problem. The prosecutor on your case wants to know who Peck is. She found out your sister has been talking to him, believes he hired me, and discovered he was your childhood friend."

"So what, why is she interested in Peck?"

Murphy unfolded his arms. "Lamont Tyne, the kid---Mad Dog, who shot at you and killed the little boy, showed up at a dinner party with a firebomb the prosecutor and the victim's mother were attending."

"What!"

Murphy nodded. "Yes, a firebomb, cocktail, or whatever you want to call it. His intentions it appears, were to burn down the house with the people inside."

"What does this have to do with Peck?"

"The dinner was at a house two doors from your sister. She knew about the dinner party, and she was aware the prosecutor and the little boy's mother would be among the guests."

Tommie frowned. "I still don't know what this has to do with my sister or Peck."

"The prosecutor believes your sister gave Peck the address, and he gave it to Mad Dog."

Tommie sat back in his chair thinking how he told Sheila to be careful what she told Glenn. He looked at Murphy with a sullen face. "What will happen to my sister?"

"Patty, I mean the prosecutor wants to know who your friend Peck is, and if she doesn't get this information, your sister could be in trouble and additional charges could be placed against you."

"Why is my sister in trouble? She didn't do anything wrong, and how could more charges be brought against me?" Tommie asked as he sat on the edge of his chair. He threw up his hands, "I didn't have nothing to do with what went down last night, and I didn't shoot Mr. Joe or that kid. Mad Dog was shooting at me, and I was almost killed!" Tommie said smacking the top of the table.

"You shot back at him Mr. Jenkins, and you had drugs in your car when arrested above the amount considered for personal consumption."

"It was just marijuana."

"Still against the law, and Patty is playing hardball. She's threatening to turn your case over to federal court. You could be charged with murder in the furtherance of a drug conspiracy."

Tommie sat back in his chair and shook his head. His mind ventured to the day he delivered weed to Colby at the barbershop. He normally did not deal drugs in west Baltimore but he made an exception for his friend. If he had not gone to that side of town, maybe that little boy could still be alive. He faced his attorney and asked, "Why not tell her who Peck is?"

"I don't think I can represent you if Peck becomes a person of interest in that attempted firebombing. It could be a conflict of interest."

"What you mean is you would dump me and represent him."

"I don't work for free Mr. Jenkins."

Before Tommie could comment further, he heard the gate slide open. An attractive woman and a thin, tall, man entered the room. The woman looked as if she stepped out of one of those magazines Tommie saw at the checkout counter in the supermarket.

"Good afternoon Ms. Lagrue," Murphy said standing.

Tommie noticed his attorney's light brown face reddened and realized the woman had to be the prosecutor.

"This is Detective Hollis," Ms. Lagrue said as she approached Murphy. "I believe you two have met?"

"Yes, we have on several occasions," Murphy, answered as he shook the detective's hand.

They did not acknowledge Tommie. He felt invisible and wondered if he should have the guards take him back to his cell.

"What's your client's answer?" the prosecutor asked and pulled out a chair and sat at the table.

Murphy gave her a half smile. "Are you even authorized to offer my client a deal since you are second chair on this case?" He sat back and crossed his legs. "In addition, the person who shot the two victims is now dead. Remember, he died trying to throw a firebomb at a house you were in."

Tommie glared at Murphy. His attorney had not told him Mad Dog was dead. This was the most aggressive Tommie had seen Murphy, and he was not sure it was a good idea. He could see anger brewing on the prosecutor's face.

She stood, pointed her finger at Murphy, and yelled, "I could've been killed last night." She pounded the table with her closed fist. "I don't have time to waste. If I didn't have authority, I wouldn't be here! Sean, if you're gonna ask silly questions, I'll just meet the United States Attorney early Monday morning and ask him to take on this case." She continued pointing her finger, "After I tell him a murder occurred during a drug transaction, your client could face up to twenty years or longer in federal prison."

Tommie felt his heart beating fast upon hearing he could spend most of his life in jail. He could not believe the bad exchange between the prosecutor and Murphy. It did not escape him they were on first name basis.

His attorney held out his hand. "I'm sorry, Patty. That's unnecessary. We both know the treatment facing my client. Black defendants don't stand a chance in that court, especially if they're male. You have put me in a difficult situation..."

"His name is Glenn Peck," Tommie said, speaking for the first time since the prosecutor and detective entered the room. "Glenn was married to Priscilla Bolt, whose father was the head of the Thrifty Bank."

"Did she die around eight months ago at the Arch Hotel?" Detective Hollis inquired.

"Yes, that's the night I saw Glenn after thirty years. We were kids together, but back then his name was Brian Adams."

The prosecutor and detective looked at each other.

Patty said to Tommie, "Continue."

Murphy interrupted his client and asked, "If he tells you everything he knows concerning Peck, what's your offer?

"I won't go to the feds, and I'll take the murder charge off the table. He'll have to plead guilty to possession with intent to distribute and discharging a firearm in the city limits."

"Come on Patty, all he had on him was marijuana."

"He had too much for personal use, and as far as I know marijuana is still illegal in this state."

"What about my sister?" Tommie asked.

"She's safe. I won't charge her with any crimes."

Satisfied with the response, Tommie told the prosecutor everything he knew about his old childhood friend. He described what Glenn told him about the kidnapping, the Pecks dying in a fire, and what he knew about the night Glenn's wife died. No one in the room spoke as Tommie gave very vivid details. The prosecutor may have ignored him when she first came in the room, but now she appeared to hang onto his every word.

He paused, "I can't believe Glenn gave Mad Dog the address of the party, but if he did, it was not to hurt you or that little boy's mother. He don't care about either of you, or helping me."

"If he doesn't care what happens to you, why would he get you an attorney?" The prosecutor asked.

"It's his way of paying a debt and keeping tabs on me. Glenn's biggest concern is losing his lifestyle. He don't want no one questioning who he is. Other than me, the only other person who is a threat to blowing his game is his Aunt Pearl."

The prosecutor jumped out of her seat and leaned across the table toward Tommie. Her face was so close he could smell her minty-scented breath.

"Tell me everything you know about his Aunt Pearl."

Tommie could tell he had hit a nerve by mentioning Glenn's aunt. The prosecutor's fists clenched, lips trembled, and her eyes widened.

"His Aunt Pearl was friends with my late cousin and was at my house when I was a boy. She was crying and my cousin was trying to calm her after her sister died and the Pecks took her nephew. I was around seven, but I'd never seen anyone cry that hard. To this day, I ain't seen pain that deep."

The prosecutor sat back in her chair, took a deep breath, and closed her eyes. It was so quiet in the room, Tommie could hear the noise of other inmates yelling to each other, and the gate opening and closing in the background. She opened her eyes after a few seconds that seemed to Tommie closer to several minutes, and looked at Murphy, "Come to my office tomorrow and pick up the plea agreement." She walked to the gate with the detective on her heels. The guards opened the gate, and the two exited the center in silence.

Once they reached their car, Ray asked, "What's going on, Patty?"

Joyce A. Smith

"Aunt Pearl told me she thought Glenn was her nephew, and I dismissed her."

"I know how you feel. I wish I had followed my instincts the night Peck's wife died. There should have been an investigation."

"You were there?"

Ray nodded. "Her death always bothered me. I couldn't understand why her nitroglycerin pill was so far from her body. I don't believe she tried to take it and it rolled or bounced clear across the room. I also don't believe she dropped something so important, and not know it, or failed to pick it up, but the family was prominent and she had a documented heart condition so the case was closed as natural causes."

"I know Glenn, and never liked him, but I didn't think him capable of violence...."

Ray's phone rang interrupting Patty. Jay was screaming, Sheila's been kidnapped.

CHAPTER 37

Glenn sat in the van in front of Asia's house listening to Sheila crying. He turned to her and shouted, "Will you please shut-up. I can't think with you crying like a baby."

Tears soaked her face as she turned to her brother's childhood friend and yelled, "I hate you. I wish I never called you."

Sheila's captor pulled back his pocket so she could see his gun, and warned through clenched teeth, "I'm telling you for the last time, shut-up!" He got out of the van, walked to the side, opened the door, retrieved the plant, the bag containing the tape, and wrench set. Glenn held the plant with one hand with the strap of the bag over his shoulder, approached the passenger side, and told Sheila to get out.

Glenn exhaled and said in a calm tone, "Take the plant, hold it to the side of your body, walk up the front steps, and ring the doorbell. Don't try anything cute because I'm right behind you."

Sheila did as directed while Glenn hid behind her and the plant. He recognized his aunt's voice as she answered the door and thought back to how his aunt was there for him and his mother. His heart skipped a beat, and for a brief second he thought about leaving and getting back into the van. *I've come too far and can't turn back now.* Pearl opened the front door to greet Sheila; he pulled out his gun and pushed his captive into the house. Pearl jumped as Glenn pointed the gun and told her to be quiet.

"Who else is in the house with you?" he asked.

"Who are you and what do you want?"

"You know who I am." Brian took off his sunglasses so she could get a clear view.

"Oh my goodness, Brian, I knew it was you when we were in Boston. If you knew it was me, why'd you pretend not to know me, and why have you pushed your way into my home with a gun pointed at me?"

"Where's Asia and Mike?"

"In the kitchen, why are you pointing a gun at me?" Pearl asked again.

"Lead the way Aunt Pearl," he said ignoring her questions.

Glenn followed Pearl and Sheila into the kitchen and was impressed at the beauty of his aunt's home.

"Who's that at the door, Pearl?" Mike asked as soon as she entered the kitchen.

But before she could answer, Glenn pushed Sheila into the kitchen and told everyone to stay calm.

Mike stood screaming, "Who the hell are you, and what do you want?"

Sweat dripped from Glenn's forehead. "Do as you're told and no one gets hurt," he said with his voice shaking.

"You're the man we met at Winston's house. If you think we have any money, you're sadly mistaken."

"That's Brian," Pearl explained.

"Yes, it's me in the flesh, thirty years older."

"Wait a minute, what do you want? I know this can't be because your Aunt couldn't find you thirty years ago," Mike said pointing his finger at Glenn. "She tried everything in her power to find you."

"Sit down old man before I shoot you."

"What is this about?" Pearl asked. "Why are you doing this to us? We're family."

"I knew you recognized me in Boston. If not, I knew it wouldn't be long before you did. I can't have people asking questions about me. Don't you understand?"

"No, I don't understand," Pearl answered. "Why would you come here threatening us with a gun?"

"Look at me," Glenn shouted. I have a good life. In fact a great life, and I can't let you or anyone interrupt what I worked to accomplish!"

"We don't want or need anything from you," Mike answered. "So what you going to do son shoot four people?"

"I'm not your son, and no, I won't shoot you."

"Sheila will tape all of you to your chairs and I will tape her last." The phone rang, and Glenn walked to the phone, while still pointing his gun at them, and pulled the cord out of the wall.

"Then I'll disconnect the stove," he said as if

there had not been an interruption. "The gas from the disconnected pipe will make you all go to sleep." He retrieved the rolls of duct tape from his bag. "It will be painless, I promise."

"Are you crazy?" Mike shouted. "You could blow up this entire block!"

"So, would you rather I shoot you? I have to go through all this trouble over a little boy dying at a barbershop. I bet the kid wouldn't have grown up to be worth much anyway."

***

Asia had not spoken a word since Glenn entered the kitchen. She sat at the end of the table, inches from him as he spoke those cruel words about her son. His words opened a wound in her, which had not yet healed. Asia thought back to sitting on the barbershop floor, holding and rocking her deceased child. She remembered the vivid and unforgettable cries of the young man who killed her son as he was on the ground burning and crying for his mother. She felt a stabbing pain in her chest and intense anger boiled from her stomach. Asia had never felt such rage; it consumed her as a hot fire.

She leapt out of her chair with such force she knocked Glenn into the stove and landed on top of him as he hit the floor. The gun he held discharged and a sharp pain pierced her body. The fury within her was so intense; she ignored the pain.

Asia grabbed Glenn's head and pounded it against the stove he planned to use to kill her family and her friend. She saw the shocked expression on his face as he attempted to push her away, but she was relentless. She felt arms pulling her; but she would not let go of Glenn's head and continued banging it against the stove.

Asia heard a boy's voice. It was soft, but became louder, saying, "I love you this much Mommy." She let go of Glenn's head, and heard his voice again, "I love you this much Mommy." Asia was sure it was Eric's voice but how was it possible? She remembered the game they played where they'd held their arms open while professing their love for each other. Asia got off Glenn, sat on the floor, and opened her arms. "I love you this much," she said.

Glenn was on the floor crying and bleeding. Uncle Mike kicked the gun away and held him down with a chair, while Pearl and Sheila knelt beside Asia. Sheila grabbed the dishtowel and applied pressure to Asia's side, trying to stop the bleeding.

"I heard Eric. I heard my baby," Asia said before she passed out.

CHAPTER 38

Asia opened her eyes, saw the tubes connected to her arm, and realized she was in the hospital. She looked around and saw her aunt and uncle sleeping in chairs next to her bed.

She tried to move, but felt a sharp pain in her side so severe she could not stifle her moans.

Mike and Pearl woke up at once.

"How are you?" her aunt asked, holding her hand.

"I feel pain in my side. What happened---how are you two, where's Sheila and Glenn or Brian, whatever his name?" Asia asked in one breath.

"You were shot, and we're fine." Mike said as he stroked Asia forehead. "Sheila's in the waiting room with Patty, Thelma, Ray, Jay, and the kids. The man who shot you is also in the hospital, but he's on his way to jail."

"I don't remember being shot. Everything's fuzzy in my head."

"Glenn shot you," Mike continued. "His gun discharged after you knocked him against the stove. You charged him like a superwoman," he chuckled. "The doctor said you were lucky the bullet went straight through you, and it didn't hit a major artery or any organs, but you will still be in considerable pain while healing."

Pearl let out a sigh. "Now you're awake, I'll call the nurse for pain medication."

"Wait, I want to tell you both something before I take any pain killers. I heard Eric. I know I wasn't imaging it. His voice was clear."

Pearl smiled, "You heard him because he lives in your heart. As long as you love him, he'll never die."

Mike wrapped his arms around his wife's waist as he spoke with his niece. "The doctors and nurses will be glad you're awake. Your friends are driving them crazy. Thelma asks the nurse every five minutes to check your vitals, and your doctor doesn't know whether to run from Patty or ask her for a date. Jay and Ray are the only ones not harassing the hospital staff. They've sat in the waiting room all day, looking into each other's eyes." Mike smiled and shook his head.

"What happened after I passed out?"

"Ray and Patty arrived at the house within minutes after you were shot, followed by other police officers."

"How did they arrive so soon?"

"It was a combination of things that led them to our door. We didn't answer the phone, and Patty knew we were usually home on Sunday afternoons. Thelma saw a man we now know was Glenn, put Sheila in a van; and Sheila's brother gave Patty and Ray some information concerning *that* man and Pearl."

"I'm so sorry this all happened," Pearl said in a somber tone. "Drink this, honey," she said picking up a cup of water and putting a straw in it for Asia.

"This is not your fault," Mike said to his wife.

"If I had found him when he was little, maybe he would've turned out different."

"You tried, and that's all you could do."

"This may not the best time to say this, but I could never abandon him."

"Pearl, for crying out loud! That man tried to kill us because he's afraid we'd blow his cover."

"I know it won't be easy, but at some point we have to forgive him, not for him but for us."

Mike grumbled. "I'll cross that bridge on a cold day in hell."

Asia smiled in spite of the pain. *Uncle Mike sure knows how to put things.* She looked at her aunt and uncle, "We make choices in life, good and bad, but we're responsible for our own actions." The pain in her side was getting much stronger and Asia knew she would soon need pain medication. "I'm not going to Boston. My place is here helping kids in my community."

"How'd you think Patty's friend will react when he finds out you're not coming?" Pearl asked.

"Of course, he'll be disappointed," answered Mike. "He's got money, and will have to find someone else." Mike took Asia's hand, "I'm glad you're not going to Boston. I was not happy with that decision."

"I know Uncle Mike, but at the time I thought it could be a new start for me. I know now I was trying to run from my pain."

She wanted to tell them of her plans to go back to school, get a degree in early childhood education, and turn the barbershop where her son died into an early learning center named Eric's Place. She had been thinking about these plans for several weeks, but the recent turn of events helped convince her.

Asia continued, "I can't bring Eric back, but maybe I can help another child. This may be the best way to honor Eric's memory."

Pearl smiled, holding Asia's hand. "Helping other children would be such a great testimony.

"Thank you, Aunt Pearl." Wincing from pain Asia added, "It's time to call the nurse."

***

Asia kept her eyes closed as she listened to Patty talking to the handsome Dr. John Drake. She could tell Patty was attracted to him, and it was interesting to hear Patty flirting with him. The doctor became professional when Asia opened her eyes. She wanted to laugh and tell him it was too late she had seen the big grin on his face.

"Oh Asia, you're awake. I was sitting here while Aunt Pearl and Uncle Mike went to get a bite. I'll leave while Dr. Drake attends to you," Patty smiled at the doctor. "I'll be back when he finishes."

Asia nodded at Patty. If she were not still in pain, she would have laughed. She observed the doctor as he inspected her wound. He had a fine chiseled-brown face, with a smile that should make any patient feel better, and she hoped Patty had found someone special.

Dr. Drake finished his examination, and Asia asked him to tell Patty to come back later as she was tired and needed to rest. She smiled, hoping the doctor had sense enough to take advantage of the time.

Asia closed her eyes and reflected on all that had happened to her in the last few months. She felt teary, but refused to cry. She was tired of crying. It was time to be strong for herself and the memory of her sweet son. Asia was not sure how she could survive, but she knew she had to not only survive, but also flourish. It was time she took charge of her life. The thought of going back to school frightened her. She had not been the best student. School was something she did because she had too, but now she was ready to give it all she had.

She knew her plans to open an early learning center for young boys was ambitious, but she felt determined and with help from her friends and family believed she could achieve her goal.

Asia thought of Patty and Dr. Drake and wondered if she would ever find love. As determined as she felt about her plans, there was a void in her life. She longed for the soft touch of someone who cared for her, with all her faults and imperfections. She told herself to forget about love and concentrate on her plans. Love was not something for everyone, especially not people like her.

She heard a sound, opened her eyes, and saw the hospital door opening to her room. Coming towards her was a rainbow-colored bouquet of roses. Smiling and carrying the beautiful array of flowers was Winston Augustus. Asia hoped her monitors did not beep, as she was so glad to see him. Maybe there was an expectation of love in her future.

EPILOGUE

The grand opening of Eric's Place was on the sixth anniversary of the death of Asia's son. The decorations for the celebration included a huge picture of Eric, surrounded by blue and white balloons. There was live music, appetizers, soft drinks, and ample seating.

Asia thought it could be hard work opening this center, but as difficult as getting her degree and a teaching job were, they paled compared to opening Eric's Place in Joe's old barbershop.

She sat on the stage waiting for her turn to speak and scanned the audience. She saw Patty, her husband, John, and their three-year-old son, Eric Raizel. The biggest allocation of funds for the center came from Dr. John Drake as he secured an endowment from the hospital where he was one of the top chief surgeons. Catching Patty's eye, Asia smiled as she continued to scan the audience.

Asia smiled when she spotted Ray and Jay. Married for four years, Jay was expecting a girl in two months, and Ray sat holding his wife's hand beaming.

Asia and Augustus kept in touch even after she did not go to Boston. After over a year of communications between the two of them, Augustus applied and obtained a nice position with a major university in Baltimore City. Uncle Mike told Asia, Augustus applied for the position and brought his family to Baltimore for her, not for a job. To her relief and joy, Augustus and Uncle Mike had become good friends.

Ray Jr., his sister, Kiki, Win, and Marcus were sitting in the back of the room giggling and whispering. Asia felt so much joy watching Win behave as a young man instead of Lizzie's great protector, he no longer reminded Asia of a ninja robot. Lizzie sat on the front row so close to Aunt Pearl they appeared to be one body. Pearl was a major influence on Lizzie and gave the child the one thing no professional could---unconditional love.

Sheila and Thelma came into the center together and waived at Asia. Tommie came home around a year ago, and John helped Sheila get her brother a job in the hospital. Asia heard Tommie and Thelma had been dating for several months. Sheila's secret drug-dealing brother had become a good man and friend to Thelma's son, Marcus. Asia was glad Tommie had turned his life around and was there for Marcus, but she was not ready to accept him, maybe in time, she thought.

Glenn changed his name back to Brian Adams. It was more of a formality because his name was not legally changed. The court sentenced Brian to a mental health lock-down facility instead of prison based on the findings of mental defect. Brian lost his position at the bank. To pay his legal fees, he had to sell his house, jewelry, cars, and liquidated most of his other assets---the things he had fought so hard to protect.

Pearl kept her promise not to abandon her nephew. She was the only one that went to the hospital to visit him. Mike drove her there every Sunday and patiently waited for her in the car, as hell must have been still hot in his mind.

Brian still had most of his inheritance, and despite Ray's suspicion, there was no evidence to tie Brian to Priscilla's death or any other crimes except trying to kill Asia, her friend, and family. Brian gave his aunt the ability to manage his inheritance, and Pearl tried to get Asia to take a donation. She argued it was for the children, and Brian's road to redemption; however, Asia would not give in to her request. The center could use the money, but Asia assured Pearl that she had not forgiven him; and did not want to send mixed messages by accepting his money.

Asia had not forgiven him, but she did pity him. She could not understand how he could go to such drastic lengths and be prepared to kill four people to protect a life-style. Maybe he was mentally disturbed, or was that what a lack of love could do. Asia wished he had come clean the day they met at Augustus' house, or left them alone.

She heard Brian had been writing Sheila, asking for her forgiveness. He offered to help pay for Sheila to go back to school and get her RN license. Asia prayed that her friend made the correct decision on accepting either his apology and or his money.

Walter entered the center without Brenda. Asia was surprised to see him as she had not seen him since her son's funeral, and hoped one day she would see her Aunt Brenda again. Asia neglected to invite her father to Eric's Place's grand opening because she forgot about him.

A woman peeked in the front window and Asia wondered why the woman did not come in and take a seat. At first, she did not recognize the woman, upon looking harder Asia realized it was Mad Dog's mother.

Several weeks prior to Eric's place opening, Tisha came to Mike and Pearl's house and told Pearl she had been drug-free since her son died, and had obtained a cleaning job working for Colonel James. She gave Pearl an envelope and told her it was for the center. In the envelope was two-hundred dollars. Pearl told Asia, "It was money that didn't go into Tisha's arm."

It was Asia's turn to speak. She looked at her husband, Augustus, and gave a silent prayer of thanks for the love and support he had given her. They built a strong friendship before they got married, and for several years, he avoided her in a romantic way. She was ready to give up hope when he asked her out on the day of her graduation from college.

She was glad they waited. It gave her time to grow-up and become a strong woman in her own rights. It also prepared her for the challenges they could face as a multi-racial blended family. They had been married for a year, and she now knew what real love was.

Standing at the podium, she felt Eric in her heart. He was a major part of her, as her breath, her heartbeat---and always would be. The joy of having Eric was now greater than the sorrow of losing him.

Asia started to speak when Ericka, her six-month-old unborn child, moved in her stomach. *Wait my angel your time will be here soon.*

CUTS DEEPER

Asia's father entered and sat at the rear of the center. He caught his daughter's eye and waived at her. Mike turned, saw Walter, frowned, and whispered to a man sitting beside him.

Walter heard his daughter had married and wondered if the man Mike spoke to was her new husband. Asia did not invite her father to her wedding, and it bothered him that Mike was probably the one who walked her down the aisle, but Walter could not be upset, as he had not been in Asia's life.

His daughter had matured and was more beautiful than the last time he saw her six years ago at Eric's funeral. Walter noticed the gentle bump in her stomach and wondered how many months it would be before her child entered the world. He looked at the giant picture of Eric surrounded by blue and white balloons and hoped he would have an opportunity to meet his new grandchild.

Asia was at the podium speaking about the purpose of Eric's Place, but Walter's mind was on events that happened several hours before he came to the celebration. He had blood on his hands, and he wondered if it would soon spill over onto his daughter.

Part II Coming Soon!

About the Author

Joyce A Smith was born and raised in Baltimore, Maryland. She graduated from the University of Baltimore with a Bachelor's degree in Business Administration. She was employed by Baltimore City in the Police Department and the State's Attorney's Office for a total of thirteen years. She retired from the United States District Court after twenty-seven years. She resides in Baltimore, MD with her husband. To learn more about the author, please visit storytellingpublishers@gmail.com.

32722721R00133

Made in the USA
Middletown, DE
15 June 2016